PROM NIGHTS FROM HELL

PROM NIGHTS FROM

Hell

MEG CABOT

KIM HARRISON

MICHELE JAFFE

STEPHENIE MEYER

LAUREN MYRACLE

HARPER**TEEN**

An Imprint of HarperCollinsPublishers

HarperTeen is an imprint of HarperCollins Publishers.

Prom Nights from Hell
"The Exterminator's Daughter" copyright © 2007 by Meg Cabot LLC.
"The Corsage" copyright © 2007 by Lauren Myracle
"Madison Avery and the Dim Reaper" copyright © 2007 by Kim Harrison
"Kiss and Tell" copyright © 2007 by Michele Jaffe
"Hell on Earth" copyright © 2007 by Stephenie Meyer

Library of Congress Cataloging-in-Publication Data is available.
ISBN-10: 0-06-125309-X — ISBN-13: 978-0-06-125309-6

Typography by Amy Ryan
❖
First HarperTeen edition, 2007

A portion of the proceeds from the sale of this collection will be donated to First Book.

First Book is an international nonprofit organization with a single mission: to give children from low-income families the opportunity to read and own their first new books. Through hundreds of local Advisory Boards, the First Book National Book Bank, and the First Book Marketplace, the organization provides an ongoing supply of new books to children participating in community-based mentoring, tutoring, and family literacy programs. First Book has provided more than 46 million new books to children in need in thousands of communities nation-wide. For more information about First Book, please visit www.firstbook.org or call 866-393-1222.

PROM NIGHTS FROM HELL

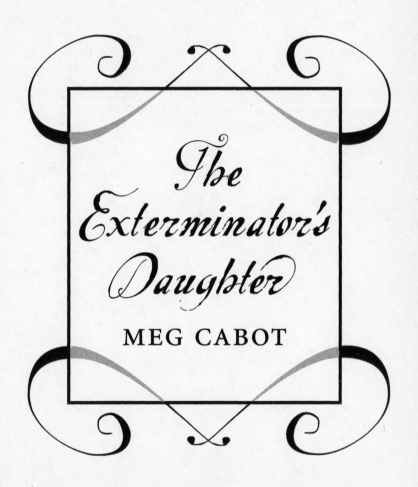

The Exterminator's Daughter

MEG CABOT

Mary

THE MUSIC IS POUNDING in time to my heartbeat. I can feel the bass in my chest—*badoom, badoom.* It's hard to see across the room of writhing bodies, especially with the fog from the dry ice, and the flickering light show coming down from the club's industrial ceiling overhead.

But I know he's here. I can feel him.

Which is why I'm grateful for the bodies grinding against one another all around me. They're keeping me hidden from his view—and from his senses. Otherwise he'd have smelled me coming by now. They can detect the scent of fear from yards away.

Not that I'm scared. Because I'm not.

Well. Maybe a little.

But I have my Excalibur Vixen crossbow 285 FPS

with me, with a twenty-inch-long Easton XX75 (the tip, formerly gold, now replaced with hand-carved ash) already cocked and ready to be released at the merest pressure from my finger.

He'll never know what hit him.

And, hopefully, neither will she.

The important thing is to get a clean shot—which won't be easy in this crowd—and to make it count. I'll probably only get one chance to shoot. Either I'll hit the target . . . or he'll hit me.

"Always aim for the chest," Mom used to say. "It's the largest part of the body, and the spot you're least likely to miss. Of course, you're more likely to kill than wound if you aim for the chest rather than the thigh or arm . . . but what do you want to wound for, anyway? The point is to take 'em down."

Which is what I'm here to do tonight. Take 'im down.

Lila will hate me, of course, if she figures out what really happened . . . and that it was me who did it.

But what does she expect? She can't think that I'm just going to sit idly by and watch her throw her life away.

"I met this guy," she'd gushed at lunch today, while we were standing in line for the salad bar. "Oh my God, Mary, you wouldn't believe how cute he is. His name's Sebastian. He's got the bluest eyes you've ever seen."

The thing about Lila that a lot of people don't get is

that beneath that—let's face it—slutty exterior beats the heart of a truly loyal friend. Unlike the rest of the girls at Saint Eligius, Lila's never pulled an attitude with me about the fact that my dad's not a CEO or plastic surgeon.

And yeah, okay, I have to tune out about three-fourths of what she says because most of it is stuff that I have no interest in—like how much she paid for her Prada tote at the end-of-season clearance sale at Saks, and what kind of tramp stamp she's thinking about getting next time she's in Cancún.

But this caught my attention.

"Lila," I said. "What about Ted?"

Because Ted's all Lila has talked about for the past year, ever since he finally got up the guts to ask her out. Well, I mean, all she's talked about besides the Prada sales and back tattoos.

"Oh, that's over," Lila said, reaching for the lettuce tongs. "Sebastian's taking me clubbing tonight—at Swig. He says he can get us in—he's on the VIP list."

It wasn't the fact that this guy, whoever he was, claimed to be on the VIP list of the newest and most exclusive club in downtown Manhattan that caused the hairs on the back of my neck to rise. Don't get me wrong—Lila's beautiful. If anyone is going to be approached by a random stranger who happens to be on the most sought-after VIP list in town, it would be Lila.

It was the thing about Ted that got to me. Because

Lila adores Ted. They're the quintessentially perfect high school couple. She's gorgeous, he's a star athlete . . . it's a match made in teen heaven.

Which is why what she was telling me did not compute.

"Lila, how can you say it's over between you and Ted?" I demanded. "You two have been going out forever"—or at least since I arrived at Saint Eligius Prep in September, where Lila was the first (and, to date, pretty much the only) girl in any of my classes to actually speak to me—"and it's the prom this weekend."

"I know," Lila said, with a happy sigh. "Sebastian's taking me."

"Seb—"

That's when I knew. I mean, *really* knew.

"Lila," I said. "Look at me."

Lila looked down at me—I'm small. But, as Mom used to say, I'm fast—and I saw it at once. What I should have seen from the beginning, that ever-so-slightly glazed expression—the dull eyes . . . the soft lips—that I've come to know so well over the years.

I couldn't believe it. He'd gotten to my best friend. My *only* friend.

Well. What was I supposed to do? Sit back and let him take her?

Not this time.

You'd think seeing a girl with a crossbow on the

dance floor of Manhattan's hottest new club would maybe generate a comment or two. But it *is* Manhattan, after all. Besides, everyone is having too good a time to notice me. Even—

Oh God. It's him. I can't believe I'm finally seeing him in the flesh. . . .

Well, his son, anyway.

He's more handsome than I ever imagined. Golden-haired and blue-eyed, with movie star–perfect lips and shoulders a mile wide. He's tall, too—although most guys are tall—compared with me.

Still, if he is anything like his father, well, then, I get it. I finally get it.

I guess. I still don't—

Oh God. He's sensed my gaze. He's turning this way—

It's now or never. I raise my bow:

Good-bye, Sebastian Drake. Good-bye forever.

But just as I have the bright white triangle of his shirt front in my scope, something unbelievable happens: A bright bloom of cherry red appears exactly where I've been aiming.

Except I haven't pulled the trigger.

And his kind doesn't bleed.

"What's that, Sebastian?" Lila shimmies up to him to ask.

"Dammit! Somebody"—and I see Sebastian raise his

stunned cerulean gaze from the scarlet stain on his shirt to Lila's face—"*shot* me."

It's true. Someone *has* shot him.

Only it wasn't me.

And that's not all that doesn't make sense. He's *bleeding*.

Except that's not possible.

Not knowing what else to do, I duck behind a nearby pillar, pressing the Vixen to my chest. I need to regroup, figure out my next move. Because none of this can really be happening. I couldn't have been wrong about him. I did the research. It all makes sense . . . the fact that he's here in Manhattan . . . the fact that he went after my best friend, of all people . . . Lila's dazed expression . . . everything.

Everything except what just happened.

And I had just stood there, staring. I had had a perfect shot, and I'd blown it.

Or had I? If he's bleeding, then that must mean he's human. Doesn't it?

Except if he's human, and he's just been shot in the chest, *why is he still standing*?

Oh God.

The worst of it is . . . he saw me. I'm almost sure I felt that reptilian gaze pass over me. What will he do now? Will he come after me? If he does, it's all my own fault. Mom *told* me never to do this. She always said a hunter never goes out alone. Why didn't I listen? What was I *thinking*?

That's the problem, of course. I hadn't been thinking at all. I'd let my emotions get the better of me. I couldn't let what happened to Mom happen to Lila.

And now I'm going to pay for it.

Just like Mom.

Crouching in agony, I try not to imagine what Dad's going to do when the New York City police ring our doorbell at four in the morning and ask him to come to the morgue to ID his only daughter's body. My throat will be gouged open, and who knows what other atrocities will be done to my broken body. All because I didn't stay home tonight to work on my paper for Mrs. Gregory's fourth-period U.S. History class (topic: the temperance movement in antebellum Civil War America, two thousand words, double-spaced, due Monday), like I was supposed to.

The music changes. I hear Lila squeal, "Where are you going?"

Oh God. He's coming.

And he wants me to know that he's coming. He's playing with me now . . . just like his father played with Mom, before he . . . well, did what he did to her.

Then I hear a strange sound—a sort of *whoosh*—followed by another "Dammit!"

What is happening?

"Sebastian." Lila's voice sounds bemused. "Someone is shooting *ketchup* at you!"

What? Did she just say . . . *ketchup*?

And then, as I carefully turn to try to get a look past the pillar to see what Lila is talking about, I see him.

Not Sebastian. His shooter.

And I can hardly believe my eyes.

What's *he* doing here?

Adam

It's all ted's fault. He's the one who said we should follow them on their date.

I was like, "Why?"

"'Cause the dude's trouble, man," Ted said.

Except there's no way Ted could have known that. Drake had basically turned up from out of nowhere outside Lila's Park Avenue apartment building just the night before. Ted had never even met him. How could he know anything about the guy? Anything at all?

But when I mentioned this, Ted said, "Dude, have you *looked* at him?"

I have to admit, the T Man has a point. I mean, the guy looks like he walked straight out of an Abercrombie & Fitch catalog or something. You can't trust a guy who's that, well, *perfect*.

Still, I'm not down with following other guys around. It's not cool. Even if, like Ted said, it was just to make sure Lila didn't get into trouble. I know Lila is Ted's lady—ex-lady now, thanks to Drake.

And okay, she's never been the shiniest fork in the drawer.

But following her on this date with the dude she's hooked up with? That just seemed like a bigger waste of time than—well, that two thousand–word, double-spaced essay I've got due in Mrs. Gregory's U.S. History class on Monday.

Then Ted had to go and suggest I bring the Beretta 9mm.

The thing is, even though it's just a water pistol, toy guns that look as real as that are illegal in Manhattan.

So I haven't really had an opportunity to use mine much. Which Ted knows.

And is probably why he kept going on about how freaking hilarious it would be if we soaked the guy. Because he knew I wouldn't be able to resist.

The ketchup was my idea.

And, yeah, it *is* pretty juvenile.

But what the hell else am I going to do on a Friday night? It beats a U.S. History paper.

Anyway, I told the T Man I guessed I'd be down with his plan. So long as I was the one who got to do the shooting. Which was fine with Ted.

"I just gotta know, man," he'd said, shaking his head. "Know what?"

"What this Sebastian dude's got," he said, "that I don't."

I could've told him, of course. I mean, it's pretty obvious to anyone who freaking looks at Drake what he's got that Ted doesn't. Ted's a decent-looking guy and all, but Abercrombie material he is not.

Still, I didn't say anything. Because the T Man was really hurtin' over this one. And I could sort of understand why. Lila's just one of those girls, you know? All big brown eyes and big, well, other parts, too.

But I won't go there on account of my sister, Veronica, who says I need to stop thinking of women as sex objects and start thinking of them as future partners in the inevitable struggle to survive in postapocalyptic America (which Veronica's writing her senior thesis on because she feels the apocalypse is going to occur sometime in the next decade, due to the country's current state of religious fanaticism and environmental recklessness, both of which were present at the fall of Rome and various other societies that no longer exist).

So that's how me and the T Man ended up at Swig—fortunately, Ted's uncle Vinnie is their liquor distributor, which is how we got in, and without having to go through the metal detector like everybody else—shooting ketchup at Sebastian Drake with my Beretta 9mm water pistol. I know I was supposed to be home doing that paper for Mrs. Gregory, but a guy's got to have some fun, right?

And it *was* fun to see those red stains spurting all over the guy's chest. The T Man was actually laughing for the first time since Lila sent him that text message during lunch, telling him that he was on his own for the prom, because she was going with Drake.

Everything was going great . . . until I saw Drake staring at that pillar over to one side of the dance floor. Which didn't make any sense. You'd have thought he'd have been looking over at *us*, in our VIP booth (thanks, Uncle Vinnie), considering that's the direction the ketchup assault was coming from.

That's when I noticed there was somebody hiding behind it. The pillar, I mean.

Not just *any* somebody, either, but Mary, that new girl from my U.S. History class, the one who never talks to anybody but Lila.

And she was holding a crossbow.

A *crossbow*.

How the hell did she get a crossbow through the metal detector? No way does she know Ted's uncle Vinnie.

Not that it matters. All that matters is that Drake's staring at the pillar Mary's crouched behind like he can see straight through it. There's something about the way he's looking over at her that makes me . . . well, all I know is that is *not* where I want that guy looking.

"Moron," I mutter. Mostly about Drake. But also about myself, a little. And then I aim and shoot once more.

"Oh, snap," Ted yells happily. "Did you see that? Right in the ass!"

That gets Drake's attention, all right. He turns . . .

. . . and suddenly, I get what they mean about blazing eyes. You know, in Stephen King books, or whatever? I never thought I'd actually see a pair.

But that's exactly what Drake's got, as he stares at us. Eyes that are most definitely blazing.

Come on, I find myself thinking in Drake's direction. *That's right. Come on over here, Drake. You wanna fight? I've got a lot more than just ketchup, dude.*

Which isn't exactly true. But it doesn't end up mattering, because Drake doesn't come over anyway.

Instead, he disappears.

I don't mean that he turns around and leaves the club.

I mean that one minute he's standing there, and the next he's . . . well, he's just gone. For a second the fog from the dry ice seems to get thicker—and when it clears, Lila is dancing by herself.

"Here," I say, thrusting the Beretta into Ted's hand.

"What the—" Ted scans the dance floor. "Where'd he go?"

But I've already taken off.

"Grab Lila," I yell back at Ted. "And meet me out front."

Ted utters some pretty choice expletives after that, but no one even notices. The music's too loud, and everyone's having too good a time. I mean, if they didn't notice us *shooting* at some dude with a ketchup-filled water gun—or a few seconds later, that dude literally vanishing into thin air—they're hardly likely to notice Ted shouting the F word.

I reach the pillar and look down.

She's there, panting as if she's just run a marathon or something. She's got the crossbow clutched to her chest like a kid's security blanket. Her face is as white as note-book paper.

"Hey," I say to her, gently. I don't want to startle her.

But I do anyway. She practically jumps out of her skin at the sound of my voice and turns wide, frightened eyes up at me.

"Hey, take it easy," I say. "He's gone. Okay?"

"He's gone?" Her eyes—green as the Great Lawn in Central Park in May—stare up at me. And there's no missing the terror in them. "How—what?"

"He just vanished," I say with a shrug. "I saw him looking at you. So I shot him."

"You *what*?"

I can see that the terror has disappeared as suddenly

as Drake did. But unlike with Drake, there's something in its place: anger. Mary is *mad.*

"Oh my God, Adam," she says. "Have you lost your mind? Do you have any idea who that guy even *is*?"

"Yeah," I say. The truth is, Mary's pretty cute when she's mad. I can't believe I never noticed before. Well, I guess I've never seen her get mad. There's not a lot to get all heated up about in Mrs. Gregory's class. "Lila's new man. That guy's such a loser. Did you get a look at his pants?"

Mary just shakes her head.

"What are you doing here?" she asks me in a slightly stunned voice.

"Same thing as you, apparently," I say, eyeing the crossbow. "Only you've got way more firepower. Where'd you *get* that? Are those even legal in Manhattan?"

"You're one to talk," she says, meaning the Beretta.

I hold up both hands in an I-surrender sort of way. "Hey, it was just ketchup. But that's definitely not a suction cup I see on the end of that thing. You could do some major damage—"

"That's the idea," Mary says.

And there's so much animosity—Mom keeps encouraging Veronica and me to instead use descriptive language to express ourselves—in her voice, that I *know*. I just know.

Drake's her ex.

I have to admit, I feel sort of weird when I realize this. I mean, I like Mary. You can tell she's pretty smart—she's always done the reading when Mrs. Gregory calls on her—and the truth is, the fact that she hangs around Lila, dim as she is, proves at least she's not a snob, since most of the girls at Saint Eligius won't give Lila the time of day . . . ever since that cell-phone photo went all around school of exactly what she and Ted were doing in the bathroom at that loft party downtown.

Not that there's anything wrong with what they were doing, if you ask me.

Still. I'm kind of disappointed. I'd have thought a girl like Mary would have better taste than to go out with a guy like Sebastian Drake.

Which I guess goes to prove that what Veronica's always saying about me is right: What I don't know about girls could fill the East River.

Mary

I CAN'T BELIEVE THIS. I mean, that I'm standing in the alley next to Swig, talking to Adam Blum, who sits behind me in Mrs. Gregory's fourth-period U.S. History. Not to mention Teddy Hancock, Adam's best friend.

And Lila's ex.

Whom Lila is currently steadfastly ignoring.

I've taken the ash-tipped arrow from the stock and slipped it back into my case. There will be, I know now, no extermination tonight.

Although I suppose I should be grateful that *I* wasn't the one who got snuffed out. If it hadn't been for Adam . . . well, I wouldn't be standing here right now, trying to explain to him something that's . . . well, frankly inexplicable.

"Seriously, Mary." Adam is regarding me with somber brown eyes. Funny that I'd never noticed how good-looking he is before now. Oh, he's no Sebastian Drake. Adam's hair is as dark as mine and his irises are dark as syrup, not blue as the sea.

But he does fairly well for himself with his broad-shouldered swimmer's physique—he's led Saint Eligius Prep to the regional finals in the butterfly two years in a row—and a six-foot frame (so tall that I practically have to crane my neck to see up into his face, my own height being a sadly disappointing—to me, anyway—five feet). He's a more than middling student and popular, too, if you count all the freshman girls who swoon every time he passes them in the hallway (not that he seems to notice).

There's nothing inattentive about the way he's staring at me now, though.

"What's the deal?" he wants to know, one of his thick dark eyebrows lifted with suspicion as he eyes me. "I know why Ted hates Drake. He stole his girl. But what's *your* beef with him?"

"It's personal," I say to him. God, this is so *unprofessional*. Mom will kill me when she finds out.

If she ever finds out.

On the other hand . . . well, Adam probably *did* just save my life. Even if he doesn't know it. Drake would have eviscerated me—right there in front of everyone—

without thinking twice about it.

Unless he decided to play with me first. Which, knowing his father, is exactly what he would have done.

I owe Adam. Big-time.

But I'm not about to let him know it.

"How'd you get in there?" Adam wants to know. "Don't even tell me you made it through the metal detector with that thing."

"Of course I didn't," I say. Seriously, boys are so silly sometimes. "I got in through the skylight."

"On the *roof*?"

"That is generally where they keep skylights," I point out to him.

"You're so immature," Lila is saying to Ted. Her voice is soft and breathy, even if what she's saying isn't. She can't help it, though. She's just caught in Drake's spell. "What on earth were you hoping to accomplish?"

"You've barely known this guy a *day*, Lila." Ted's got his hands shoved deep in his pockets. He looks ashamed of himself . . . but defiant at the same time. "I mean, *I* could've gotten you into Swig if that's where you'd wanted to go. Why didn't you tell me? You know about my uncle Vinnie."

"It's not about what clubs Sebastian can get me into, Ted," Lila is saying. "It's about . . . well, just him. He's . . . perfect."

I have to swallow hard to keep down the vomit that's

risen into my throat.

"Nobody's perfect, Li," Ted says, before I have a chance to.

"Sebastian is," Lila enthuses, her dark eyes glittering in the light from the single bulb illuminating the club's emergency side door. "He's so beautiful . . . and intelligent . . . and worldly . . . and gentle—"

That's it. I've heard more than I can take.

"Lila," I snap. "Shut *up*. Ted's right. You don't even know the guy. Because if you did, you'd never call him gentle."

"But he is," Lila insists, the glitter in her eyes fading to a warm glow. "You don't even know—"

A second later—I'm not even sure how it happened— I have her by the shoulders, and I'm shaking her. She's six inches taller than me and outweighs me by a good forty pounds.

But that doesn't matter. In that moment, all I want to do is knock some intelligence into her.

"He told you, didn't he?" I hear myself yell at her, hoarsely. "He told you what he is. Oh, Lila. You *idiot*. You stupid, *stupid* girl."

"Whoa." Adam is trying to pry my hands off Lila's bare shoulders. "Hey, now. Let's all calm down—"

But Lila wrenches herself out of my grasp and whirls on us with a triumphant expression.

"Yes," she cries with that exultant throb in her voice I

recognize only too well. "He told me. And he warned me about people like you, Mary. People who don't under-stand—*can't* understand—that he comes from a line as ancient and as noble as any king's—"

"Oh my God." I'm itching to slap her. The only rea-son I don't is because Adam reaches out and grabs me by the arm—almost as if he'd read my mind. "Lila. You knew? *And you went out with him anyway?*"

"Of course I did," Lila says with a sniff. "Unlike you, Mary, I have an open mind. I'm not prejudiced against his kind, the way you are—"

"His kind? His *kind*?" If it wasn't for Adam holding me back—and murmuring, *Hey, take it easy*—I'd have thrown myself at her and attempted to beat some com-mon sense into her vapid blond head. "And did he happen to mention how *his kind* survives? What they eat—or should I say *drink*—to live?"

Lila looks contemptuous. "Yes," she says. "He did. And I think you're making way too big a deal out of it. He only drinks blood he buys from a plasma center. He doesn't *kill*—"

"Oh, Lila!" I can't believe what I'm hearing. Well, I mean, I can, considering that it's Lila. Still, I would have thought that even she wouldn't be naive enough to fall for that one. "That's what they all say. They've been feed-ing that line to girls for centuries. *I don't kill humans.* It's total b.s."

"Hold on." Adam's grip on my arm has gotten quite a bit looser. Unfortunately, now that I'm at liberty to do so, I don't feel like smacking Lila anymore. I'm too disgusted. "What's going on here?" Adam wants to know. "Who drinks blood? Are you talking about—*Drake*?"

"Yes, Drake," I say tersely.

Adam stares down at me in disbelief, while beside him, his friend Ted whistles.

"Man," Ted says. "I knew there was something I didn't like about that guy."

"Stop it!" Lila cries. "All of you! Listen to yourselves! Do you have any idea how bigoted you sound? Yes, Sebastian is a vampire—but that doesn't mean he hasn't got the right to exist!"

"Uh," I say. "Considering that he's a walking abomination to humankind and has been feeding on innocent girls like you for centuries, actually, he *doesn't* have the right to exist."

"Wait a minute." Adam is still looking incredulous. "A *vampire*? Come on. That's impossible. There's no such thing as vampires."

"Oh!" Lila whirls toward him and stamps a foot. "You're even worse than they are!"

"Lila," I say, ignoring Adam. "You can't see him again."

"*He didn't do anything wrong,*" Lila insists. "He hasn't even bitten me—even though I've asked him to. He says it's because he *loves* me too much."

"Oh my God," I say in disgust. "That's just another line he's feeding you, Lila. Don't you see? They *all* say that. And he *doesn't* love you. Or at least, he doesn't love you any more than a tick loves the dog it's feeding off of."

"*I* love you," Ted says, his voice cracking on the word *I*. "And you dumped me for a *vampire*?"

"You don't understand." Lila tosses back her long blond hair. "He's not a tick, Mary. Sebastian loves me too much to bite me. But I know I can change his mind. Because he wants to be with me forever, as much as I want to be with him forever. I *know* it. And after tomorrow night, we *will* be together forever."

"What's tomorrow night?" Adam wants to know.

"The prom," I say woodenly.

"Right," Lila prattles on. "Sebastian's taking me. And though he doesn't know it yet, he's going to give in to me there. Just one bite and I'll have eternal life. Come on, you guys, how cool is that? Wouldn't you want to live forever? I mean, if you could?"

"Not that way," I say. Something inside of me aches. Aches for Lila, and aches for all the girls who've gone before her. And will come after her, too, if I don't do something about it.

"He's meeting you at the dance?" I force myself to ask her. It's hard to speak, because all I want to do is cry.

"Right," Lila says. Her face still has the same vacant

expression she wore inside the club, as well as earlier today in the lunchroom. "He'll never be able to resist me—not in my new Roberto Cavalli gown, with my neck all exposed beneath the silver light of the full moon . . ."

"I think I'm going to throw up," Ted volunteers.

"No, you're not," I say. "You're going to take Lila home. Here." I reach into my satchel and pull out a crucifix and two containers of holy water, then hand them to him. "If Drake shows up—although I don't think he will—throw these at him. Then get yourself home, after you've dropped off Lila."

Ted looks down at what I've shoved into his hands. "Wait. That's it?" he wants to know. "We're just going to let him *kill* her?"

"Not kill," Lila corrects him cheerfully. "*Turn* me. Into one of his kind."

"*We* aren't going to do anything," I say. "You guys are going to go home and leave this to me. I've got it under control. Just make sure Lila gets back safely. She should be all right until the dance. *Evil spirits cannot enter an inhabited house unless invited.*" I narrow my eyes at Lila. "You didn't invite him inside, did you?"

"Whatever," Lila says, tossing her head. "Like my dad wouldn't go *too* ballistic if he found a guy in my room."

"See? Go home. You, too," I add, to Adam.

Ted takes Lila by the arm and begins to lead her away.

But Adam, to my surprise, stays where he is, his hands buried deep in his pockets.

"Um," I say to him. "Is there something I can do for you?"

"Yes," Adam says calmly. "You can start at the beginning. I want to know *everything*. Because if what you're telling me is true, if it weren't for me, you'd be a speck on the wall in the club back there. So start talking."

Adam

IF YOU HAD TOLD me just an hour or two ago that I'd be ending my evening with a trip to Mary-from-U.S.-History-class's penthouse apartment over in the East Seventies . . . well, I'd have told you that you were high.

But that's exactly where I find myself, following Mary past her sleepy doorman (who doesn't raise so much as an eyebrow at her crossbow), and then up the elevator to her place, which is decorated in mid-nineteenth-century Victorian chic—at least as near as I can judge, considering all the furniture looks like it came out of one of those boring miniseries my mom likes to watch on PBS, featuring girls named Violet or Hortense or whatever.

There are books *everywhere*—and not Dan Brown paperbacks, either, but big, heavy books, with titles like

Demonology in Seventh-century Greece and *A Guide to Necromancy*. I look around, but I don't see a plasma screen or an LCD. Not even a regular TV.

"Are your parents professors or something?" I ask Mary as she throws down the crossbow and heads to the kitchen, where she pulls open the fridge and reaches for two Cokes, one of which she hands to me.

"Something like that," Mary says. This is what she's been like the whole way to her place: not exactly brimming with the explanations.

Not that it matters, though, since I already told her I'm not leaving until I get the whole story. The thing is, I really don't know what to think about all this so far. On the one hand, I'm relieved Drake isn't who I thought he was—Mary's ex-boyfriend. On the other hand . . . a *vampire*?

"Come on," Mary says, and I follow her because . . . well, what else am I supposed to do? I don't know what I'm doing here. I don't believe in vampires. I think Lila's just gotten herself involved with one of those freaky goth dudes I saw on *Law & Order* that one time.

Although Mary's question—"Then how do you explain his disappearance from the dance floor into thin air like that?"—bugs me. How *did* the guy do that?

Then again, there are tons of questions like that one that I don't have the answers for. Like this new one that occurred to me: How can I get Mary to look at me the way Lila looked at that guy, Drake?

Life is full of mysteries, as my dad likes to say, many of which are also wrapped up in enigmas.

Mary leads me down a dark hallway toward a partly open door, from which light spills. She taps on the door, then says, "Dad? Can we come in?"

A gruff voice says, "By all means."

And I follow Mary into the strangest room I've ever seen. At least in a penthouse apartment on the Upper East Side.

It's a laboratory. There are test tubes and beakers and vials everywhere. Standing in front of some of them is a tall, white-haired-professor type in a bathrobe, messing around with a concoction in a clear container that's bright green and vigorously generating large amounts of smoke. The old dude looks up from this and smiles as Mary comes into the room, his green-eyed gaze—a lot like Mary's—darting toward me curiously.

"Well, hello," the guy says. "I see you've brought a friend home. I'm so glad. I've been thinking lately that you spend far too much time alone, young lady."

"Dad, this is Adam," Mary says casually. "He sits behind me in U.S. History. We're going to my room to do homework."

"How nice," Mary's father says. It doesn't seem to occur to him that the last thing a guy my age is likely to be doing in a girl's bedroom at two in the morning is homework. "Don't study too hard, now, children."

"We won't," Mary says. "Come on, Adam."

"Good night, sir," I say to Mary's dad, who beams at me before turning back to his smoking beaker.

"Okay," I say to Mary as she leads me down the hall once more, this time to her room . . . which is surprisingly utilitarian for a girl's bedroom, containing only a large bed, a dresser, and a desk. Unlike in Veronica's room, everything is put away, except for a laptop and an MP3 player. I take a quick look at Mary's play list when she's busy rifling around in the closet for something. Mostly rock, some R&B, and a little rap. No emo, though. Thank God. "What's going on? What's your dad doing with all that stuff?"

"Looking for a cure," Mary says from the closet, her voice muffled.

I've moved across the ornate Persian carpet toward her bed. There's a framed photo on her nightstand. It's of a pretty woman, squinting into the sunlight and smiling. Mary's mother. I don't know how I know it. I just do.

"A cure for what?" I ask, picking up the photo for a closer look. Yep, there they are. Mary's lips. Which, I haven't been able to stop noticing, are kind of curled up at the ends. Even when she's mad.

"Vampirism," Mary says. She emerges from the closet holding a long red dress. It's wrapped in clear plastic from the dry cleaner's.

"Uh," I say, "I hate to be the one to tell you this, Mary. But there's no such thing as vampires. Or vampirism. Or whatever it is."

"Oh yeah?" The ends of Mary's mouth are curled up even more than usual.

"Vampires were just made up by that guy." She's laughing at me. I don't mind, though, because it's Mary. It's better than her ignoring me, which is what she's done for most of the time I've known her. "That guy who wrote *Dracula*. Right?"

"Bram Stoker did not make up vampires," Mary says, the smile vanishing. "He didn't even make up Dracula. Who's an actual historical figure, by the way."

"Yeah, but a dude who drinks blood and can turn into a bat? Come on."

"Vampires exist, Adam," Mary says quietly. I like how she says my name. I like it so much that I don't even notice at first that she's staring at the photo I'm holding. "And so do their victims."

I follow the direction of her gaze. And nearly drop the photo.

"Mary," I say. Because it's all I can think of to say. "Your . . . your mom? Is she . . . did she . . ."

"She's still alive," Mary says, turning to throw the red dress, in its slippery clear plastic bag, onto the bed. "If you can call it living," she adds, almost to herself.

"Mary . . . ," I say in a different tone of voice. I can't believe it.

And yet I do. There's something in her face that makes it clear she's not lying. Also something that makes me long to wrap her in my arms. Which Veronica would say is sexist. But there you go.

I let go of the lip I've started chewing. "Is that why your dad—"

"He wasn't always like that," she says, not looking at me. "He used to be different, when Mom was here. He . . . he thinks he can find a chemical cure for it." She sinks onto the bed beside the dress. "He doesn't want to believe that there's only one way to get her back. And that's killing the vampire who made her into one."

"Drake," I say, sinking down onto the bed beside her. It all makes sense now. I guess.

"No," Mary says with a quick shake of her head. "His father. Who happened to stick with the original family name of Dracula. His son just thinks Drake sounds a little less pretentious and more modern."

"So . . . why were you trying to kill Dracula's kid, if his dad is the one who . . ." I can't even bring myself to say it. Fortunately, I don't have to.

Mary's shoulders are hunched. "If killing his only kid doesn't get Dracula to come out of hiding so I can kill him, too, I don't know what will."

"Won't that be, uh . . . kind of dangerous?" I ask. I

can't believe I'm sitting here talking about this. But I can't believe I'm in Mary-from-U.S.-History's bedroom, either. "I mean, isn't Dracula, like, the head of the whole operation?"

"Yes," Mary says, looking down at the photo I've laid between us. "And when he's gone, Mom will finally be free."

And Mary's dad won't have to worry about finding a cure for vampirism anymore, I think, but don't say out loud.

"Why didn't Drake just, uh, turn Lila tonight?" I ask. Because this has been bothering me. Among other things. "I mean, back at the club?"

"Because he likes to play with his food," Mary says emotionlessly. "Just like his dad."

I shudder. I can't help it. Even though she's not exactly my type, it's not pleasant to think of Lila as some vampire's midnight snack.

"Aren't you worried," I ask, hoping to change the subject a little, "that Lila's just going to tell Drake not to show up at the prom since we'll be there waiting?"

I say *we* and not *you* because there is no way I'm letting Mary go after this guy alone. Which I know Veronica would think is sexist, too.

But Veronica's never seen Mary smile.

"Are you kidding me?" Mary asks. She doesn't seem

to notice the *we*. "I'm *counting* on her telling him. That way he'll show up for sure."

I stare at her. "Why would he do that?"

"Because killing the exterminator's daughter will totally raise his crypt cred."

Now I'm blinking at her. "Crypt cred?"

"You know," she says, tossing her ponytail. "It's like street cred. Only among the undead."

"Oh." Strangely, this does make sense. As much as anything else I've heard this evening. "They call your dad the, um, 'exterminator'?" I'm having a hard time picturing Mary's dad wielding a crossbow the way she did.

"No," she says, the smile vanishing. "My mom. At least . . . she used to be. Not just vampires, either, but evil entities of all kinds—demons, werewolves, poltergeists, ghosts, warlocks, genies, satyrs, loki, shedus, vetelas, titans, leprechauns—"

"Leprechauns?" I echo in disbelief.

But Mary simply shrugs. "If it was evil, Mom killed it. She just had a gift for it. . . . A gift," Mary adds softly, "I really hope I've inherited."

I just sit there for a minute. I have to admit I'm a little stunned by everything that's gone down over the past couple of hours. Crossbows and vampires and exterminators? And what in the world is a vetela? I'm not even sure I want to know. No. Wait. I *know* I don't want to know. There's a humming noise inside my head that won't stop.

The weird thing is, I kind of like it.

"So," Mary says, lifting her gaze to meet mine. "Do you believe me now?"

"I believe you," I say. What I can't believe, actually, is that I do. Believe her, I mean.

"Good," she says. "It would probably be better if you didn't tell anybody. Now, if you don't mind, I need to start getting things ready—"

"Great. Tell me what you need me to do."

Her face clouds with trouble. "Adam," she says. And there's something about the way her lips form my name that makes me feel a little crazy . . . like I want to throw my arms around her and race around the room at the same time. "I appreciate the offer. I really do. But it's too dangerous. If I kill Drake—"

"*When* you kill him," I correct her.

"—chances are, his father is going to show up," she goes on, "looking for revenge. Maybe not tonight. And maybe not tomorrow. But soon. And when he does . . . it isn't going to be pretty. It's going to be awful. A night-mare. It's going to be—"

"Apocalyptic," I finish for her, a slight shiver going down my spine as I speak the word.

"Yes. Yes, exactly."

"Don't worry," I say, ignoring the shiver. "I'm all set for that."

"Adam." She shakes her head. "You don't understand. I can't—well, I can't guarantee I'll be able to protect you. And I certainly can't let you risk your life like that. It's different for me, because—well, because of my mom. But you—"

I stop her. "Just tell me what time I'm picking you up."

She stares at me. "What?"

"Sorry," I say. "But you're not going to the prom by yourself. End of story."

And I must have looked really scary or something as I said it, because even though she opens her mouth to argue, she closes it again when she gets a look at my face, and only says, "Um. Okay."

Still, she has to add, "It's your funeral," just to have the last word.

Which is fine with me. She can have the last word.

Because I know now that I've found her: my future partner in the inevitable struggle to survive in post-apocalyptic America.

Mary

THE MUSIC IS POUNDING in time to my heartbeat. I can feel the bass in my chest—*badoom, badoom.* It's hard to see across the room of writhing bodies, especially with the flickering light show coming down from the ballroom's ceiling.

But I know he's here. I can feel him.

And then I see him, moving across the dance floor toward me. He's holding two glasses of bloodred liquid, one in either hand. When he gets close enough, he hands me one of the glasses, then says, "Don't worry, it's not spiked. I checked."

I don't reply. I just sip the punch, grateful for the liquid—even if it is a little too sweet—because my throat is so dry.

The thing is, I know I'm making a mistake. Letting

Adam do this, I mean.

But . . . there's something about him. I don't know what it is. Something that sets him apart from all the rest of the dumb jocks in school. Maybe it's the way he saved me back at the club when I lost my nerve, his shooting at Sebastian Drake—progeny of the devil himself—with a ketchup-filled squirt gun.

Or maybe it's the way he was so nice about my dad, not cracking any jokes about him being like Doc from the *Back to the Future* movies and even calling him *sir*. Or the way he picked up my mom's photo like that and seemed so stunned when I told him the truth about her.

Or maybe it's just the way he looked when he showed up at quarter to eight this evening, so impossibly handsome in his tux—and even holding a red rose corsage for me . . . despite that less than twenty-four hours ago, he hadn't even known he was going to the prom (good thing tickets were available for sale at the door).

Oh well. Dad was ecstatic, for once acting like a normal parent, snapping photos—"For your mother to see, when she's better," he kept saying—and trying to slip twenty-dollar bills into Adam's hand, telling him to "treat Mary to an ice cream after the dance."

Which frankly made me decide I like Dad better when he never comes out of the lab.

Still. I knew I was making a mistake by not sending Adam packing right away. This is no job for amateurs.

This is . . . this is . . .

. . . beautiful. I mean, that's how the ballroom looks. I almost gasped when I entered it on Adam's arm. (He insisted. So we'd look like a "normal couple" if Drake was there already and watching.) The Saint Eligius Prep prom committee really outdid themselves this year.

Securing the four-story grand ballroom at the Waldorf-Astoria was a feat all on its own, but transforming it into such a sparkling romantic wonderland? Miraculous.

I just hope all those rosettes and streamers are fire-proof. I'd hate to see them go up in the flames that are bound to appear when Drake's corpse begins to self-conflagrate after I stab him in the chest.

"So," Adam says, as we stand on the edge of the dance floor, sipping our punch in a silence that's—to be frank—quickly gotten a little uncomfortable. "How's this going to go down, anyway? I don't see your cross-bow anywhere."

"I'm just going with a stake," I say, showing him my leg through the slit up the side of my gown. I'd strapped a hand-carved piece of ash there, using Mom's old thigh holster. "Keeping it sweet and simple."

"Oh," Adam says, after choking on his punch a little. "Okay."

I realize he hasn't looked away from my inner thigh. I hastily lower my skirt.

And it occurs to me—for the first time—that Adam might be in this for reasons other than wanting to liberate his best friend's girlfriend from the spell of a blood-sucking fiend.

Except . . . can such a thing even be possible? I mean, he's *Adam Blum*. And I'm just the new girl. He likes me, sure, but he doesn't *like* me. He can't. I've probably only got about ten minutes left to live. Unless something radically alters what I'm pretty sure is about to go down.

Blushing, I keep my gaze on the gyrating couples in front of us. Mrs. Gregory from U.S. History is one of the chaperones. She's going around, trying to keep girls from grinding on their dates. She might as well try to keep the moon from rising.

"It'd probably be best if you kept Lila busy," I say, hoping he doesn't notice that my cheeks are now as scarlet as my gown, "while I'm doing the staking. We don't want her throwing herself in my path just to try to save him."

"That's what I dragged Ted here for," Adam says, nodding toward Teddy Hancock, who's sitting slumped at a nearby table, looking out at the dance floor in a bored manner. Like the rest of us, he's just waiting for Lila—and her date—to arrive.

"Still," I say. "I don't want you anywhere near me when . . . you know."

"I heard you the first nine million times you told

me," Adam mutters. "I *know* you can take care of yourself, Mary. You've made that abundantly clear."

I can't help wincing a little. He's not having a good
time. I can tell.

Well, so what? I didn't ask him to come! He invited
himself! This isn't a date, anyway! It's a slaying! He knew
that from the outset. He's the one changing the rules,
not me. I mean, who am I kidding? I can't *date*. I have a
legacy to fulfill. I'm the exterminator's daughter. I have
to—

"Want to dance?" Adam startles me by asking.

"Oh," I say, with some surprise. "I'd love to. But I
really should—"

"Great," he says and takes me into his arms, steering
me onto the dance floor.

I'm too stunned to do anything to stop him, really.
Well, okay, as the initial shock of it is wearing off, I find
I don't *want* to stop him. I'm stunned to realize that . . .
well, I like how it feels, being in Adam's arms. It feels
good. It feels safe. It feels warm. It feels . . . well, almost
as if I were a normal girl, for a change.

Not the new girl. Not the exterminator's daughter.
Just . . . me. Mary.

It's a feeling I could get used to.

"Mary," Adam says. He's so much taller than me that
his breath tickles the tendrils that have fallen from the
updo that I've twisted my hair into. I don't mind,

though, because his breath smells good.

I look up at him dreamily. I can't believe I never noticed—*really* noticed—how handsome he is before now. Well, last night, actually. Or maybe I noticed, but it never really registered, because what would a guy like him ever see in a girl like me? In a million years, I never thought I'd end up at the prom with Adam Blum. . . .

And okay, sure, he only asked me because he obviously feels sorry for me, on account of my mother being a vampire and all. But still.

"Hmmm?" I say, smiling up at him.

"Uh." Adam seems uncomfortable, for some reason. "I was wondering if—you know, when this is all over, and you've dusted Drake, and Lila and Ted are back together—you'd want to, um . . ."

Oh God. What's happening? Is he . . . is he about to *ask me out*? Like on a real date? One that doesn't include sharp, pointy objects?

No. This isn't happening. This is a dream or something. In a minute, I'm going to wake up, and it's all going to go away. Because how could such a thing even be possible? I can't breathe, I'm so sure I'll break whatever spell we're both under if I do. . . .

"Yes, Adam?" I ask.

"Well." He can't seem to make eye contact anymore. "Just if you'd want to, you know, maybe hang out—"

"Excuse me." The deep voice that interrupts Adam

then is all too familiar. "But may I have this dance?"

I close my eyes in frustration. I cannot believe this. I am *never* going to get a guy I actually like to ask me out at this rate. Never. Never. *Never.* I am going to stay a freak—the product of similar freaks—for the rest of my life. Why would a guy like Adam Blum ever want to go out with me in the first place? The child of a vampire and a mad scientist? Let's face it. Not going to happen.

And I've had it. I've had it up to *here.*

"Listen, you," I say, whirling around to face Sebastian Drake, whose blue eyes widen a little at the fire in mine. "How dare you come oozing around . . ."

But then my voice trails off. Because suddenly all I can see are those eyes . . .

. . . those hypnotically blue eyes, which suddenly make me feel like I could dive into them, letting their warmth wash over me in sweet, soft waves. . . .

It's true he's no Adam Blum. But he's looking at me in a way that makes it clear he knows that, and that he's sorry for it, and that he's going to do everything he can to make it up to me . . . *more* than make it up to me, even . . .

And the next thing I know, Sebastian Drake is taking me into his arms—gently, so gently—and leading me from the dance floor toward a set of French doors through which I can see a night-darkened garden, bathed in twinkling fairy lights and moonlight . . . just the kind of place to which you'd expect to be led by the golden-haired descendant of a Transylvanian count.

"I'm so glad we finally have the chance to meet," Sebastian is saying to me in a voice that seems to caress me like a feather-soft touch. Everyone and everything we've left behind us—the other couples; Adam; a stunned Lila, staring after us jealously; Ted, staring jealously at *her*; even the streamers and rosettes—seems to melt away as if all that exists in the world is me, the garden that I find myself in, and Sebastian Drake.

Who is reaching up to smooth some loose tendrils away from my face.

In a dim, inner recess of my mind, I remember that I'm supposed to be afraid of him . . . to hate him, even. Only I can't think why. How could I possibly hate someone as handsome and sweet and gentle as he is? He wants to make me feel better. He wants to help me.

"You see?" Sebastian Drake is saying, as he lifts one of my hands and presses it, softly, against his lips. "I'm not so terrifying, am I? I'm just like you, actually. Just the child of—let's face it—a very formidable person, who's trying to figure out his own place in the world. We have our burdens, do we not, you and I, Mary? Your mother says hello, by the way."

"M-my mother?" My brain seems to be as filled with fog as this garden we're standing in. Because while I can picture my mother's face, I can't remember how

Sebastian Drake could possibly know her.

"Yes," Sebastian says, his lips now moving from my hand and up toward the crook of my elbow. His mouth feels like liquid fire against my skin. "She misses you, you know. She doesn't understand why you won't join her. She's so happy now . . . she doesn't know the pain of illness . . . or the indignity of aging . . . or the heartbreak of loneliness." His lips are on my bare shoulder now. I'm having trouble breathing. But in a good way. "She is surrounded by beauty and love . . . just like you could be, Mary." His lips are by my throat. His breath, so warm, has seemed to cause my spine to go limp. But it's all right, because one of his strong arms has gone around my waist, and he's holding me up, even as my body, as if of its own volition, is arching backward, allowing him an unobstructed view of my bare throat.

"Mary," he whispers against my neck.

And I feel so peaceful, so serene—something I haven't felt in years, not since Mom left—that my eyelids drift closed. . . .

And the next thing I know, something cold and wet hits me in the neck.

"Ow," I say, opening my eyes and slapping a hand there . . . then pulling it away to find my fingers slick with some kind of clear moisture.

"Sorry," Adam calls from where he's standing a few feet away, his arms stretched out in front of him, the mouth of his Beretta 9mm water pistol aimed right at me. "I missed."

A second later, I am gasping for air as a thick cloud of acrid, burning smoke hits me in the face. Coughing, I stagger away from the man who, just seconds before, had been holding me so tenderly, but is now clutching at his smoldering chest.

"Wha—" Sebastian Drake gasps, pounding at the flames leaping from his chest. "What *is* this?"

"Just a little holy water, dude," Adam says, as he continues pumping away at Drake's chest. "Shouldn't bother you. Unless, of course, you're a member of the undead. Which, unfortunately for you, it appears you are."

And a second later, I've come back to my senses and am reaching beneath my skirt for my stake.

"Sebastian Drake," I hiss, as he sinks to his knees before me, howling in pain. And rage. *"This is for my mother."*

And I plunge the hand-carved piece of ash deep into the place where his heart would have been.

If he'd had one.

"Ted," Lila says, in a syrupy voice, as her boyfriend lies across the contoured plastic bench with his head in her lap.

"Yes?" Ted asks, looking up at her adoringly.

"No," Lila says. "That's what I'm getting for my tattoo

next time I'm in Cancún. Across the small of my back. The word *Ted*. So from now on, everyone will know I belong to you."

"Oh, *honey*," Ted says. And pulls her head down so he can stick his tongue in her mouth.

"Oh my God," I say, looking away.

"I know." Adam's returned from throwing a glow-in-the-dark twelve-pound bowling ball down the disco-lit lane. "I almost liked her better when she was under Drake's spell. But I guess it works out better this way. *Ted*'ll hurt a lot less than *Sebastian*. That was a strike, by the way. In case you missed it." He slides onto the bench beside me and looks down at the scoring sheet in the glow of the lamp just above my head. "Well, what do you know? I'm winning."

"Don't get cocky," I say. Although I have to admit, he has a lot to brag about. Not just winning at Night Strike bowling, either.

"Just tell me," I say as he reaches up and finally pulls off his bow tie. Even in the weird disco lights of Bowlmor Lanes—the bowling alley where we'd retreated for our post-prom activities, a mere nine-dollar cab ride from the Waldorf—Adam still looks obscenely handsome. "Where'd you get the holy water?"

"You gave a bunch of it to Ted," Adam says, looking down at me in some surprise. "Remember?"

"But how'd you get the idea to put it in the water gun?" I demand. I'm still reeling from the evening's earlier activities. Midnight bowling is fun and all. But nothing can really compare with slaying a two-hundred-year-old vampire at the prom.

Too bad he'd fizzled into ash out in the garden, where no one but Adam and I could see it. We'd have been voted prom king and queen for sure, instead of Lila and Ted, who are both still wearing their crowns ... although they've tilted a little rakishly, due to all the kissing.

"I don't know, Mare," Adam says, filling in his own score. "It just seemed like a good idea at the time."

Mare. No one has ever called me Mare before.

"But how did you know?" I ask. "I mean, that Drake had—well, whatever? I mean, how could you tell that I wasn't faking it? To lull him into a false sense of security?"

"You mean besides the fact that he was about to bite you on the neck?" Adam raises a single dark brow. "And that you weren't doing a damned thing to stop him? Yeah, I had a pretty good idea of what was going on."

"I'd have snapped out of it," I assure him, with a confidence I most definitely do not feel, "as soon as I felt his teeth."

"No," Adam says. Now he's grinning down at me, his face illuminated by the light from the scoring desk's single lamp. The rest of the bowling alley is in darkness, except for the balls and pins, which glow with an eerie fluorescence. "You wouldn't have. Admit it, Mary. You needed me back there."

His face is so close to mine—closer than Sebastian Drake's ever got.

Only instead of feeling as if I could dive into his gaze, I feel as if I'm about to melt under it. My heartbeat staggers.

"Yeah," I say, unable to keep my gaze from drifting toward his lips. "I guess I kinda did."

"We make a good team," Adam says. His own gaze, I can't help noticing, isn't straying far from my mouth, either. "Wouldn't you say? I mean, especially in light of the coming apocalyptic event? When Drake's dad finds out what we did tonight?"

I can't help gasping a little at that.

"That's right," I cry. "Oh, Adam! He's not just going to come after me. He's going to come after you, too!"

"You know," Adam says. And now his gaze has drifted from my mouth, and downward. "I really do like that dress. It goes great with bowling shoes."

"Adam," I say. "This is serious! Dracula could be getting ready to descend upon Manhattan at any moment, and we're wasting time *bowling*! We've got to start getting ready! We need to prepare a counterattack. We need to—"

"Mary," Adam says. "Dracula can wait."

"But—"

"Mary," Adam says. "Shut up."

And I do. Because I'm too busy kissing him back to do anything else.

Besides, he's right. Dracula can wait.

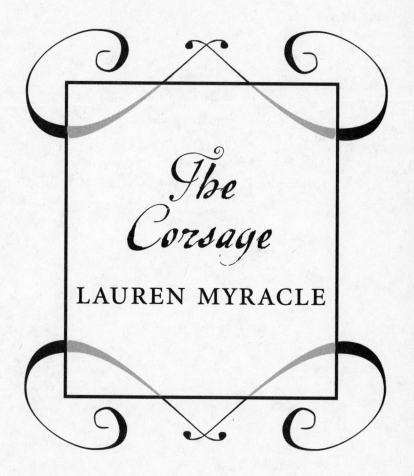

The Corsage

LAUREN MYRACLE

Readers, beware! The following story was inspired by "The Monkey's Paw," first published in 1902 by W. W. Jacobs, which scared the dickens out of me when I was a teenager. Be careful what you wish for, indeed!   —LAUREN MYRACLE

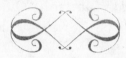

OUTSIDE, THE WIND WHIPPED around Madame Zanzibar's house, making a loose rain-pipe thump against the siding. The sky was dark, though it was only four o'clock. But within the garishly decorated waiting room, three table lamps shone brightly, each draped with a jewel-toned scarf. Ruby hues lit Yun Sun's round face, while bluish-purple hues gave Will the mottled look of someone freshly dead.

"You look like you've risen from the grave," I told him.

"Frankie," Yun Sun scolded. She did a head jerk toward Madame Z's closed office, worried, I suppose, that she might hear and be offended. A red plastic monkey hung from the office doorknob, indicating that Madame Z was with a client. We were up next.

Will made his eyes go vacant. "I am a pod person," he moaned. He stretched his arms out toward us. "Please to give me all your hearts and livers."

"Oh no! The pod person has taken over our beloved Will!" I clutched Yun Sun's arm. "Quick, give him your hearts and livers, so he'll leave mine alone!"

Yun Sun shook free. "Not amused," she said in a tone both singsongy and threatening. "And if you're not nice to me, I will leave."

"Stop being such a pooter," I said.

"I will take my thunder thighs and I will march right out of here. Just watch."

Yun Sun was on a my-legs-are-too-fat kick, just because her superslinky prom dress needed a little letting out. At least she had a prom dress. And a for-sure chance to wear it.

"Bleh," I said. Her grouchiness was endangering our plan, which was the whole reason we were here. The night of the prom was getting dangerously close, and I was not going to be the sad shell of a girl who sat home alone while everyone else went crazy with glitter dust and danced ironically in spectacular three-inch heels. I refused, especially since I knew in my heart of hearts that Will wanted to ask me. He just needed a little encouragement.

I lowered my voice, all the while smiling at Will like *la la la, just girl talk, nothing important!* "It was both of our idea to do this, Yun Sun. Remember?"

"No, Frankie, it was your idea," she said. And she did *not* keep her voice down. "I've already got my date, even though he's going to be squished to death by my thighs. You're the one hoping for a last-minute miracle."

"Yun Sun!" I glanced at Will, who turned red. Bad Yun Sun, throwing it out in the open like that. Bad, bad, naughty girl!

"Ow!" she yelped. Because I'd whacked her.

"I am very mad at you," I said.

"Enough with the coyness. You *do* want him to ask you, don't you?"

"*Ow!*"

"Um, you guys?" Will said. He was doing that adorable thing he did when he was nervous, when his Adam's apple bobbed up and down. Although, huh. That was kind of an icky image. It made me think of bobbing for apples, which was only one step away from bobbing for Adam's apples.

But. Will was indeed possessed of an Adam's apple, and when it moved up and down in his throat, it was indeed adorable. It made him look so vulnerable.

"She hit me," Yun Sun tattled.

"She deserved it," I countered. But I didn't want it to go further, this line of conversation that was already too revealing. So I patted Yun Sun's totally unfat leg and said, "However, I forgive you. Now shut up."

What Yun Sun failed to get—or more likely, what she totally got and yet failed to appreciate—was that not all things needed to be said aloud. Yes, I wanted Will to ask me to prom, and I wanted him to do it *soon*, because "Springtime Is for Lovers" was only two weeks away.

And fine, the name of the dance was dorky, but springtime *was* for lovers. It was an indisputable truth. Just as it was an indisputable truth that Will was my forever boy, if only he could get past his enduring bashfulness and make a frickin' move. Enough chummy shoulder slugs and giggling, snorting tickle wars! Enough clutching each other and shrieking, blaming it on our Netflix copies of *The Body Snatchers* or *They Come from the Hills*! Couldn't Will see that I was his for the taking?

He'd almost popped the question last weekend, I was ninety-nine-point-five percent sure. We'd been watching *Pretty Woman*, an overblown romance which never failed to amuse. Yun Sun had disappeared into the kitchen for snacks, leaving the two of us alone.

"Um, Frankie?" Will had said. His foot tap-tap-tapped against the floor, and his fingers flexed on his jeans. "Can I ask you something?"

Any fool would have known what was coming, because if he'd just wanted me to turn up the volume, he'd simply have said, "Hey, Franks, turn up the volume." Casual. Straightforward. No need for any preparatory remarks. But since there *were* preparatory remarks . . .

well, what could he possibly have wanted to ask me besides "Will you go to prom?" Eternal delight was right there, only seconds away.

And then I'd blown it. His palpable nervousness triggered a spaz-out of my own, and instead of letting the moment play out, I'd skittishly changed the subject. BECAUSE I WAS A FREAK.

"Now see, that's the way it's done!" I said, pointing at the TV. Richard Gere was galloping on his white steed, which was really a limo, to Julia Roberts's castle, which was really a crappy third-story apartment. As we watched, Richard Gere climbed out of the sun roof and scaled the fire escape, all to win the affections of his beloved.

"None of this namby-pamby 'I think you're kinda cute' baloney," I went on. I was blathering, and I knew it. "We're talking action, baby. We're talking grand gesture of love."

Will gulped. And said, "Oh." And blinked at Richard Gere in a startled-teddy-bear way, thinking, I'm sure, that he could never, ever compare.

I stared at the TV, knowing I'd sabotaged my prom night happiness through my own stupidity. I didn't care about "grand gestures of love"; I just cared about Will. But brilliant me, I'd gone and scared him off. Because in actual real reality, I was an even bigger wimp than he was.

But no more—which was why we were here at Madame Zanzibar's. She would tell us our futures, and unless she was a total hack, she would state the obvious as an impartial observer: Will and I were meant for each other. Hearing it spoken so plainly would give Will the guts to try again. He'd ask me to prom, and this time I'd let him, even if it killed me.

The plastic monkey twitched on the office doorknob.

"Look, it's moving," I whispered.

"Oooo," Will said.

A black man with snow-white hair shuffled out of the office. He had no teeth, which made the lower half of his face look puckered, like a prune.

"Children," he said, tipping his hat.

Will stood up and opened the front door, because that's the kind of guy he was. A gust of wind nearly toppled the old man, and Will steadied him.

"Whoa," Will said.

"Thank you, son," the old man replied. His words came out mushy, because of the no-teeth thing. "Reckon I best skedaddle before the storm blows in."

"I think it already has," Will said. Past the driveway, tree branches thrashed and creaked.

"This weensy old wind?" the old man said. "Aw, now, this is just a baby waking up and wanting to be fed. It'll be worse before the night is over, mark my words." He peered at us. "In fact, shouldn't you children be home, safe and sound?"

It was hard to take offense when a toothless old-timer called you "children." But come on, this was the second time in twenty seconds.

"We're juniors in high school," I said. "We can take care of ourselves."

His laugh made me think of dead leaves.

"All right, then," he said. "I'm sure you know best." He small-stepped onto the porch, and Will gave a half wave and shut the door.

"Crazy coot," came a voice from behind us. We turned to see Madame Zanzibar in the office doorway. She wore hot pink Juicy Couture sweatpants with a matching hot pink top, unzipped to her clavicle. Her breasts were round and firm and amazingly perky, given that she didn't seem to be wearing a bra. Her lipstick was bright orange, to match her nails, and so was the end of the cigarette she held between two fingers.

"So, are we coming in or are we staying out here?" she asked the three of us. "Unveiling life's mysteries or leaving well enough alone?"

I rose from my chair and pulled Yun Sun with me. Will followed. Madame Z ushered us into her office, and the three of us scrunched together in an overstuffed armchair. Will realized it was never going to work and lowered himself to the floor. I wiggled to make Yun Sun give me more room.

"See? They're sausages," she said, referring to her thighs.

"Scooch," I commanded.

"Now," Madame Z said, crossing in front of us and sitting behind a table. She puffed on her cigarette. "What's your business?"

I bit my lip. How to put it? "Well, you're a psychic, right?"

Madame Z exhaled a cloud of smoke. "Gee, Sherlock, the ad in the Yellow Pages tip you off?"

I blushed, while at the same time bristling. My question had been a conversation opener. Did she have a problem with conversation openers? Anyway, if she really was a psychic, shouldn't she already know why I was here?

"Uh . . . okay. Sure, whatever. So I guess I was wondering . . ."

"Yeah? Out with it."

I gathered my courage. "Well . . . I was wondering if a certain special person was going to ask me a certain special question." I purposefully didn't look at Will, but I heard his spurt of surprise. He hadn't seen this coming.

Madame Z pressed two fingers to her forehead and let her eyes go blank. "Ahem," she said. "Hmm, hmm. What I'm getting here is muzzy. There is passion, yes"—

Yun Sun giggled; Will swallowed audibly—"but there are also . . . how do I say? Complicating factors."

Gee, thanks, Madame Z, I thought. *Could we dig a little deeper here? Give me something to work with?*

"But is he—I mean, the person—going to *act* on his passion?" I was brazen, despite my knotted stomach.

"To act or not to act . . . that is the question?" Madame Z said.

"Yes, that is the question."

"Ahhh. That is always the question. And what one must always ask oneself—" She broke off. Her eyes flew to Will, and she paled.

"What?" I demanded.

"Nothing," she said.

"*Some*thing," I said. Her message-from-the-spirits performance wasn't fooling me. She wanted us to think she'd been suddenly possessed? That she'd had a stark and powerful vision? Fine! Just get to the bloody answer!

Madame Z made a show of pulling herself together, complete with a long, shaky draw on her cigarette. Looking dead at me, she said, "If a tree falls in a forest, and no one's there to hear it, does it still make a sound?"

"Huh?" I said.

"That's all I've got. Take it or leave it." She seemed agitated, so I took it. Although I made cuckoo eyes at Yun Sun when Madame Z wasn't watching.

Will claimed not to have a specific question, but

Madame Z was oddly insistent on relaying a message to him anyhow. She waved her hands over his aura and warned him sternly of heights, which was curiously appropriate as Will was an avid rock climber. What was more curious was Will's reaction. First his eyebrows shot up, and then a different emotion took over, like some secret anticipatory pleasure. He glanced at me and blushed.

"What's going on?" I asked. "You have your sneaky face on."

"Exsqueeze me?" he said.

"What are you not telling us, Will Goodman?"

"Nothing, I swear!"

"Don't be stupid, boy!" Madame Z harped. "Listen to what I'm saying."

"Oh, you don't have to worry about him," I said. "He's a total Mr. Safety." I turned back to Will. "For real. Do you have a fabulous new climbing spot? A brand-new shiny carabiner?"

"It's Yun Sun's turn," Will said. "Yun Sun, go."

"Can you read palms?" Yun Sun asked Madame Z.

Madame Z exhaled, and she was barely engaged as she traced her finger over the plump pad below Yun Sun's thumb. "You will be as beautiful as you allow yourself to be," she told her. That was it. Those were her pearls of wisdom.

Yun Sun seemed as underwhelmed as I was, and

I felt like protesting on all our behalves. I mean, seriously! A tree in the forest? Be careful of heights? You will be as beautiful as you allow yourself to be? Even with her somewhat convincing touches of atmospheric creepiness, the three of us were getting cheated. Me in particular.

But before I could say anything, a cell phone on the desk rang. Madame Z picked it up and used a long orange nail to punch the talk button.

"Madame Zanzibar, at your service," she said. Her expression changed as she listened to whoever was on the other end. She grew brisk and annoyed. "No, Silas. It's called a . . . yes, you can say it, a yeast infection. *Yeast* infection."

Yun Sun and I shared a glance of horror, although— I couldn't help it—I was also delighted. Not that Madame Z had a yeast infection. I mean, ick. But that she was discussing it with Silas, whoever he was, while all of us listened in. *Now* we were getting our money's worth.

"Tell the pharmacist it's the second time this month," Madame Z groused. "I need something stronger. What? For the itching, you idiot! Unless he wants to scratch it for me!" She twisted on her swivel chair, pumping one Juicy Coutured leg over the other.

Will looked up at me, his brown eyes wide with alarm. "I will not be scratching it for her," he stage-whispered. "I refuse!"

I laughed, thinking it a good sign that he was show-ing off for me. The Madame Z experience hadn't gone as intended, but who knew? Maybe it would end up having the desired effect after all.

Madame Z pointed at me with the lit end of her cig-arette, and I ducked my chin contritely, like *Sorry, sorry.* To distract myself, I focused on the strange and varied clutter on her shelves. A book called *Magic of the Ordinary* and another titled *What to Do When the Dead Speak—But You Don't Want to Listen.* I nudged Will with my knee and pointed. He mimed choking the poor deceased bastard, and I snortled.

Above the books I saw: a bottle of rat poison, an old-fashioned monocle, a jar of what looked like fingernail clippings, a stained Starbucks cup, and a rabbit's foot, claws attached. And on the shelf above that was . . . oh, lovely.

"Is that a skull?" I asked Will.

Will whistled. "Holy cannoli."

"Okey-doke," Yun Sun said, averting her eyes. "If there really is a skull, I don't want to know about it. Can we leave now?"

I took her head in my hands and pointed her in the right direction. "Look. It still has hair!"

Madame Z snapped her cell phone shut. "Fools, every one of them," she said. Her pallor was gone; appar-ently talking to Silas had shaken her out of her funk.

"Ahh! I see you found Fernando!"

"Is that whose skull that is?" I asked. "Fernando's?"

"Oh God," Yun Sun moaned.

"Wormed his way to the surface after a gully washer, out in Chapel Hill Cemetery," Madame Z told us. "His coffin, that is. Crappy wooden thing, must'a been from the early nineteen hundreds. No one left to care for him, so I took pity on him and brought him here."

"You opened the coffin?" I said.

"Yep." She seemed proud. I wondered if she'd worn her Juicy Couture during the grave robbing.

"That's gross that it still has hair," I said.

"*He* still has hair," Madame Z said. "Show some respect."

"I didn't know dead bodies had hair, that's all."

"Skin, no," Madame Z said. "Skin starts to rot right away, and believe me, you don't want to smell it when it goes. But hair? Sometimes it keeps growing for weeks after the deceased has made his crossing."

"Wowzers." I reached down and tousled Will's honey-colored curls. "Hear that, Will? Sometimes the hair keeps growing."

"Amazing," he said.

"What about that?" Yun Sun asked, pointing to a clear Tupperware container in which something reddish and organlike floated in clear liquid. "Please tell me it didn't come from Fernando, too. *Please.*"

Madame Z waved her hand, like *Don't be ridiculous.* "That's my uterus. Had the doc give it to me after my hysterectomy."

"Your uterus?" Yun Sun looked ill.

"I'm going to let 'em toss it in the incinerator?" Madame Z said. "Fat chance!"

"And that?" I pointed to a clump of dried-up something on the highest shelf. This show-and-tell was proving far more enjoyable than our actual readings.

Madame Z followed my gaze. She opened her mouth, then closed it. "That's nothing," she said firmly, although I noticed she had a hard time tearing her eyes from it. "Now. Are we done here?"

"Come on." I made praying hands. "Tell us what it is."

"You don't want to know," she said.

"I do," I said.

"*I* don't," Yun Sun said.

"Yes, she does," I said. "And so does Will. Right, Will?"

"It can't be worse than the uterus," he said.

Madame Z pressed her lips together.

"Please?" I begged.

She muttered something under her breath about idiot teenagers and how she refused to take the blame, whatever came of it. Then she stood up, pawing the top shelf. Her bosom didn't jiggle, but stayed firm and rigid beneath her top. She retrieved the clump and placed it in front of us.

"Oh," I breathed. "A corsage." Brittle rosebuds, their edges brown and papery. Sprigs of graying baby's breath, so desiccated that puffs of fiber dusted the table. A limp red ribbon holding it all together.

"A peasant woman in France put a spell on it," Madame Z said in a tone that was hard to decipher. It was as if she were compelled to speak the words, even though she didn't want to. Or, no. More like she *did* want to but was struggling to resist. "She wanted to show that true love is guided by fate, and that anyone who tries to interfere does so at her own peril."

She moved to return the corsage.

"Wait!" I cried. "How does it work? What does it do?"

"I'm not telling," she said stubbornly.

"'I'm not telling'?" I repeated. "How old are you, four?"

"Frankie!" Yun Sun said.

"You're just like all the rest, aren't you?" Madame Z said to me. "Willing to do anything for a boyfriend? Desperate for a heart-stopping romance, no matter the cost?"

I felt my face go hot. But here it was, out on the table. Boyfriends. Romance. Hope flickered in my chest.

"Just tell her," Yun Sun said, "or we'll never get to leave."

"No," Madame Z insisted.

"She can't, because she made it up," I said.

Madame Z's eyes flashed. I'd provoked her, which wasn't nice, but something told me that whatever it was, she *hadn't* made it up. And I really wanted to know.

She put the corsage in the middle of the table, where it sat doing absolutely nothing.

"Three people, three wishes apiece," Madame Z declared. "That's its magic."

Yun Sun, Will, and I looked at one another, then burst out laughing. It was ludicrous and at the same time perfect: the storm, the wacko, and now the ominously issued pronouncement.

And yet the way Madame Z regarded us made our laughter trickle off. The way she regarded Will, especially.

He tried to resurrect the hilarity.

"So, why don't you use it?" he asked in the manner of a teenager being helpful and polite.

"I did," she said. Her orange lipstick was like a stain.

"And . . . were your three wishes granted?" I asked.

"Every last one," she said flatly.

None of us knew what to say to that.

"Well, has anyone else used it?" Yun Sun asked.

"One other lady. I don't know what her first two wishes were, but her last was for death. That's how the corsage came to me."

We sat there, all silliness squelched. The situation felt unreal, yet here we were, in this moment.

"Dude, that's spooky," Will said.

"So . . . why do you keep it?" I asked. "If you've used up your three wishes?"

"Excellent question," Madame Z said after staring at the corsage for a few heavy seconds. She pulled a turquoise lighter from her pocket and struck a flame. She picked up the corsage with a fierce determination, as if committing to a course of action long overdue.

"No!" I yelped, snatching it from her grasp. "Let me have it, if you don't want it!"

"Never. It should be burned."

My fingers closed over the rose petals. They were the texture of my grandfather's wizened cheek, which I stroked when I visited him at the nursing home.

"You're making a mistake," Madame Z warned. She reached to reclaim the bundle, then jerked her hand back convulsively. I sensed the same internal warring as when I first goaded her into speaking of the corsage, as if the corsage had an element of actual power over her. Which was ridiculous, of course.

"It's not too late to change your fate," she managed.

"What fate would that be?" I said. My voice broke. "The fate where a tree falls in the forest, but poor me, I'm wearing earplugs?"

Madame Z fixed me with her thick-lashed eyes. The

skin around them was as thin as crepe paper, and I realized she was older than I originally assumed.

"You are a rude and disrespectful child. You deserve a spanking." She leaned back in her swivel chair, and I could tell—*snap*, like that—she'd released herself from the corsage's unhealthy hold. Or perhaps the corsage had done the releasing? "You keep it, that's your decision. I take no responsibility for what happens."

"How do you use it?" I asked.

She snorted.

"C'mon," I pleaded. I didn't mean to be a brat. It was just that it was so terribly important. "If you don't tell me, I'll do it all wrong. I'll probably . . . I don't know. Destroy the whole world."

"Frankie . . . let it go," Will said under his breath.

I shook my head. I couldn't.

Madame Z clucked at dim, foolish me. Well, let her.

"You hold it in your right hand and speak your wish aloud," she said. "But I'm telling you, no good will come of it."

"You don't need to be so negative," I said. "I'm not as stupid as you think."

"No, you're far more stupid," she agreed.

Will jumped in to redirect, because that's what he did. He hated all unpleasantness. "So . . . you wouldn't use it again, if you were able?"

Madame Z raised her eyebrows. "Do I look like I need more wishes?"

Yun Sun sighed loudly. "Well, *I* could sure use a wish or two. Wish me up Lindsay Lohan's thighs, will you?"

I loved my friends. They were so wonderful. I lifted the corsage, and Madame Z gasped and grabbed my wrist.

"For heaven's sake, girl," she cried. "If you're going to wish, at least make it for something sensible!"

"Yeah, Frankie," Will said. "Think of poor Lindsay— you want the girl to be thighless?"

"She'd still have her calves," I pointed out.

"But would they be attached? And what movie producer's going to hire a girl who's just a torso?"

I giggled, and Will looked pleased with himself.

Yun Sun said, "You guys. *Ew.*"

Madame Zanzibar's breathing was uneven. She might have resolved to wash her hands of me, but her fright, when I lifted the withered rosebuds, hadn't been contrived.

I placed the corsage in my messenger bag, careful not to squish it. And when I drew out my wallet, I paid Madame Z twice the amount she'd quoted. I didn't elaborate, just handed over the bills. She counted them, then assessed me in a bone-tired, orange-lipsticked way.

Fine, then, her demeanor conveyed. *Just . . . beware.*

We headed to my house for pizza, because that was our Friday night ritual. Saturdays and Sundays, too, more often than not. My parents were on sabbatical in Botswana for the semester, which meant Chez Frankie was party central. Except we didn't have actual parties. We could have; my house was miles from town on an unmaintained dirt road, with no nearby neighbors to complain. But we preferred our own company, with an occasional pop-in from Jeremy, Yun Sun's boy-friend. Jeremy thought Will and I were weird, though. He didn't like pineapple on his pizza, and he didn't share our taste in movies.

The rain pounded the roof of Will's pickup as he navigated the winding curves of Restoration Boulevard, past the Krispy Kreme and the Piggly Wiggly and the county watertower, which stretched toward the sky in lonely glory. The cab of the truck was crowded with all three of us scrunched in, but I didn't mind. I had the middle seat. Will's hand brushed my knee when he shifted gears.

"Ah, the cemetery," he said, nodding as we reached the wrought iron gates to his left. "Shall we have a moment of silence for Fernando?"

"We shall," I said.

A bolt of lightning illuminated the rows of tomb-stones, and I thought to myself what eerie and disturbing places cemeteries really were. Bones. Rotted-away skin. Coffins, which sometimes came undug.

I was glad to get home. I went from room to room flicking on all the lights while Will ordered the pizza and Yun Sun shuffled through this week's Netflix arrivals.

"Something cheerful, 'kay?" I called from the hall.

"Not *Night Stalker*?" she said.

I joined her in the den and sifted through the stack. "How about *High School Musical*? There is nothing the slightest bit creepy about *High School Musical*."

"Surely you jest," Will said, clicking off his phone. "Sharpay and her brother doing their sexy dance with maracas? You wouldn't call that creepy?"

I laughed.

"But you girls go on, knock yourselves out," he said. "I've actually got an errand to run."

"You're leaving?" Yun Sun said.

"What about the pizza?" I said.

He opened his wallet and laid a twenty-dollar bill on the coffee table. "It'll be here in thirty minutes. My treat."

Yun Sun shook her head. "And again I say: You're *leaving*? You're not even staying to eat?"

"There's something I need to do," he said.

My heart constricted. I ached to keep him here, even if just for a little longer. I darted back to the kitchen and pulled Madame Z's corsage—no, *my* corsage—out of my bag.

"At least wait till I've made my wish," I said.

He looked amused. "Fine, wish away."

I hesitated. The den was warm and cozy, pizza was on the way, and I had the two greatest friends in the world. What else did I truly want?

Duh, the grasping part of my brain told me. Prom, of course. I wanted Will to ask me to prom. Maybe it was selfish to have so much and still want more, but I pushed that line of reasoning away.

Because look at him, I thought. Those kind brown eyes, that lopsided smile. Those ridiculously angelic curls. The entire sweetness and goodness that was Will.

He hummed the *Jeopardy!* theme song. I raised the corsage.

"I wish for the boy I love to ask me to prom," I said.

"And there you have it, folks!" Will cried. He was far too euphoric. "And what boy *wouldn't* want to take her to prom, our fabulous Frankie? Now we'll just have to wait and see, won't we, whether her wish will come—"

Yun Sun cut him off. "Frankie? Are you okay?"

"It moved," I said, cringing away from the corsage, which I'd flung to the floor. My skin was clammy. "I swear to God, it moved when I made the wish. And that smell! Do you smell it?"

"Noooo," she said. "What smell?"

"You smell it, Will. Don't you?"

He grinned, still on whatever high he'd been on

since . . . well, since Madame Z warned him away from heights. A clap of thunder rumbled, and he shoved my shoulder.

"Next you're going to blame the storm on the evil wish fairies, aren't you?" he said. "Or, no! You're going to go to bed tonight, and tomorrow you'll tell us you found a hunched and skulking creature on your comforter, smiling a twisted smile!"

"Like rotting flowers," I said. "You honestly don't smell it? You're not playing with me?"

Will dug his keys out of his pocket. "See you on the flip side, homies. And, Frankie?"

"What?"

Another boom of thunder shook the house.

"Don't give up hope," he said. "Good things come to those who wait."

I watched through the window as he dashed to his truck. The rain was coming down in sheets. Then I turned to Yun Sun, a balloony feeling pushing everything else away.

"Did you hear what he said?" I grabbed her hands. "Oh my God, do you think it means what I think it means?"

"What else *could* it mean?" Yun Sun said. "He's going to ask you to prom! He's just . . . I don't know. Trying to make a big production out of it!"

"What do you think he's going to do?"

"*No* idea. Hire a skywriter? Send a singing telegram?"

I squealed. She squealed. We jumped about in a frenzy.

"Got to hand it to you, the wish thing was brilliant," she said. She flicked her finger to indicate giving Will the push he needed. "And the rotting flowers? Verrrry dramatic."

"I honestly did smell it, though," I said.

"Ha-ha."

"I did."

She looked at me and shook her head, amused. Then she looked at me again.

"Well, it must have been your imagination," she said.

"I guess," I said.

I picked the corsage up off the floor, holding it gingerly between my thumb and forefinger. I took it to the bookshelf and dropped it behind a row of books, glad to have it out of sight.

The next morning I trotted downstairs, hoping foolishly to find . . . I don't know. Hundreds of M&Ms spelling out my name? Pink hearts sketched in silly string on the windows?

Instead, I found a dead bird. Its tiny body lay on the welcome mat, as if it had flown into the door during the storm and bashed its brains in.

I scooped it up with a paper towel and tried not to

feel its soft weight as I delivered it to the outside trash bin.

"I'm sorry, little bird, so pretty and sweet," I said. "Fly to heaven." I dropped in the corpse, and the lid slammed shut with a bang.

I returned inside to the sound of the ringing phone. Probably Yun Sun, wanting an update. She'd left with Jeremy at eleven last night, after making me swear to tell her the minute Will made his bold move.

"Hey, sweetie," I said, after glancing at the caller ID and seeing that, yep, I was right. "No news yet—sorry."

"Frankie . . . ," Yun Sun said.

"I've been thinking about Madame Z, though. Her whole don't-mess-with-fate mumbo jumbo."

"Frankie—"

"Because how could Will asking me to prom lead to anything bad?" I walked to the freezer and grabbed a box of frozen waffles. "Spit's going to fly from his mouth and land on me? He'll bring me flowers, and a bee'll zip out and sting me?"

"Frankie, stop. Didn't you watch the morning news?"

"On a Saturday? I don't think so."

Yun Sun made a gulping sound.

"Yun Sun, are you *crying*?"

"Last night . . . Will climbed the watertower," she said.

"What?!" The watertower was easily three hundred

feet tall, with a sign at the bottom prohibiting anyone from ascending. Will always talked about climbing to the top, but he was such a rule-follower that he never had.

"And the railing must have been wet . . . or maybe it was lightning, they don't yet know . . ."

"Yun Sun. What happened?"

"He was spray painting something on the tower, the stupid idiot, and—"

"Spray painting? *Will?*"

"Frankie, will you shut up? He fell! He fell off the watertower!"

I gripped the phone. "Jesus. Is he okay?"

Yun Sun was unable to talk for sobbing. Which I understood, sure. Will was her friend, too. But I needed her to pull it together.

"Is he in the hospital? Can I go visit him? Yun Sun!"

There was wailing, and then a shuffling sound. Mrs. Yomiko took over.

"Will died, Frankie," she said. "The fall, the way he landed . . . he didn't make it."

"I'm sorry . . . what?"

"Chen is on his way to get you. You'll stay with us, yes? As long as you want."

"No," I said. "I mean . . . I don't . . ." The box of waffles fell from my hand. "Will didn't *die*. Will couldn't have *died*."

"Frankie," she said, her voice infinitely sad.

"Please don't say that," I said. "Please don't sound so . . ." I didn't understand how to make my mind work.

"I know you loved him. We all did."

"Just *wait*," I said. "Spray painting? Will doesn't spray paint. That's something a pothead would do, not Will."

"Let's get you to the house. We'll talk about it then."

"But what was he spray painting? I don't under-stand!"

Mrs. Yomiko didn't answer.

"Let me speak to Yun Sun," I pleaded. "Please! Put on Yun Sun!"

There was a muffled exchange. Yun Sun came back on.

"I'll tell you," she said. "But you don't want to know."

A cold feeling spread over me, and suddenly, I *didn't* want to know.

"He was spray painting a message. That's what he was up there doing." She hesitated. "It said, 'Frankie, will you go to prom with me?'"

I sank to the floor, next to a box of waffles. Why was there a box of waffles on the kitchen floor?

"Frankie?" Yun Sun said. Tinny, faraway sound. "Frankie, are you there?"

I didn't like that tinny sound. I pressed the Off button to make it go away.

Will was buried in the Chapel Hill Cemetery. I sat, numb, through the funeral, which was closed-coffin because

Will's body was too mangled to be viewed. I wanted to say good-bye, but how did you say good-bye to a box? At the grave site, I watched as Will's mother threw a handful of dirt into the hole where Will lay. It was horrible, but the horror felt distant and unreal. Yun Sun squeezed my hand. I didn't squeeze back.

It rained that evening, a gentle spring shower. I imagined the ground, damp and cool around Will's coffin. I thought of Fernando, whose skull Madame Zanzibar had liberated after his coffin shifted in the wet earth. I reminded myself that the east side of the cemetery, where Will was buried, was newer, with tidy landscaping. And of course there were modern ways of digging graves now, more efficient than men with shovels.

Will's coffin wouldn't come undug. It was impossible.

I stayed with Yun Sun for nearly two weeks. My parents were called, and they offered to return from Botswana. I told them no. What good would it do? Their presence wouldn't bring Will back.

At school, for the first few days, kids talked in hushed tones and stared at me as I passed. Some thought it was romantic, what Will did. Others thought it was stupid. "A tragedy" was the phrase most often used, spoken in mournful tones.

As for me, I haunted the halls like the living dead. I

would have ditched, but then I'd have been corralled by the counselor and forced to talk about my feelings. Which wasn't going to happen. My grief was my own, a skeleton that would rattle forever within me.

One week after Will's death, and exactly one week before prom, kids started talking less about Will and more about dresses and dinner reservations and limos. A sallow girl from Will's chemistry class got upset and said prom should be canceled, but others argued no, prom must go on. It's what Will would have wanted.

Yun Sun and I were consulted, since we were his best friends. (And since I, though they didn't say it, was the girl he died for.) Yun Sun's eyes welled with tears, but after a shaky moment, she said it would be wrong to ruin everyone's plans, that sitting home and mourning wouldn't do anyone any good.

"Life goes on," she said. Her boyfriend, Jeremy, nodded. He put his arm around her and drew her close.

Lucy, president of the prom committee, placed her hand over her heart.

"So true," she said. She turned to me with an overly solicitous expression. "What about you, Frankie? Do you think you could get behind it?"

I shrugged. "Whatever."

She embraced me, and I staggered.

"Okay, guys, we're on!" she called, bounding across

the commons. "Trixie, back to work on the cherry blossoms. Jocelyn, tell the Paper Affair lady we need a hundred blue streamers and don't take no for an answer!"

On the afternoon of the dance, two hours before Jeremy was due to pick up Yun Sun, I crammed my stuff in my duffel bag and told her I was going home.

"What?" she said. "No!" She put down a hot roller. Her makeup lay in front of her on her vanity, her Babycakes body glitter and Dewberry lip gloss, and her dress hung over the hook of her open bathroom door. It was lilac, with a sweetheart neckline. It was gorgeous.

"It's time," I said. "Thank you for letting me stay so long . . . but it's time."

Her mouth turned down. She wanted to argue, but she knew it was true. I wasn't happy here. That in itself wasn't the issue—I wasn't going to be happy anywhere—but moping around the Komikos' house was making me feel trapped and making Yun Sun feel helpless and guilty.

"But it's prom," Yun Sun said. "Won't that be weird, being alone in your house on the night of prom?" She came over to me. "Stay till tomorrow. I'll be quiet when I come in, I swear. And I promise not to go on and on about . . . you know. The after-parties and who hooked up and who passed out in the girls' bathroom."

"You *should* get to go on about that stuff, though," I said. "You should stay out as late as you want and come in as loudly as you want and be giddy and spazzy and all that." Unexpectedly, my eyes filled with tears. "You *should*, Yun Sun."

She touched my arm. I pulled away, but in what I hoped was an unobvious manner.

"So should you, Frankie," she said.

"Yeah . . . well." I heaved my bag over my shoulder.

"Call me any time," she said. "I'll keep my cell on, even at the dance."

"Okay."

"And if you change your mind, if you decide you want to stay—"

"Thanks."

"Or even if you decide to come to prom! We all want you there—you know that, right? It doesn't matter that you don't have a date."

I winced. She didn't mean it the way it sounded, but it most certainly did matter that I didn't have a date, because that date would have been Will. And I didn't have him not because he liked another girl or was suffering from a terrible case of the flu, but because he was dead. *Because of me.*

"Oh God," Yun Sun said. "Frankie . . ."

I waved her off. I didn't want any more touching. "It's all right."

We stood in a bubble of awkwardness.

"I miss him, too, you know," she said.

I nodded. Then I left.

I returned to my empty house to find that the electricity was out. Perfect. This happened more often than it should have: Afternoon thunderstorms threw tree branches into the transformers, and entire neighborhoods lost power for several hours. Or the power would go out for no reason. Maybe too many people had their air conditioners on and the circuits overloaded, that was my theory. Will's theory was ghosts, ha ha ha. "They've come to spoil your milk," he'd say in a spooky voice.

Will.

My throat tightened.

I tried not to think about him, but it was impossible, so I let him exist there with me in my mind. I fixed myself a peanut butter sandwich, which I didn't eat. I went upstairs and lay on my bed without turning down the covers. Shadows deepened. An owl hooted. I stared at my ceiling until I could no longer make out the spiderweb cracks.

In the dark, my thoughts went places they shouldn't. Fernando. Madame Zanzibar. *You're just like all the rest, aren't you? Desperate for a heart-stopping romance?*

It was that very desperation that gave birth to my stupid Madame Zanzibar plan and even stupider wish. That's what prodded Will into action. If only I'd never taken the damn corsage!

I bolted upright. Oh my God—the damn corsage!

I grabbed my cell and held down the "three," Yun Sun's speed dial. "One" was for Mom and Dad; "two" was for Will. I still hadn't deleted his name, and now I wouldn't have to.

"Yun Sun!" I cried when she answered.

"Frankie?" she said. "S.O.S." by Rihanna blared in the background. "Are you okay?"

"I'm fine," I said. "Better than fine! I mean, the power's out, it's pitch-black, and I'm all alone, but whatever. I won't be for long." I giggled and fumbled my way into the hall.

"Huh?" Yun Sun said. More noise. People laughing. "Frankie, I can hardly hear you."

"The corsage. I've got two wishes left!" I jogged downstairs, zinging with glee.

"Frankie, what are you—"

"I can bring him back, don't you get it? Everything will be good again. We can even go to prom!"

Yun Sun's voice grew sharp. "Frankie, no!"

"I'm such an *idiot*—why didn't I think of it before?"

"Wait. Don't do it, don't make the—" She broke off. I heard a "whoops," followed by drunken apologies and someone saying, "Oh, I *love* your dress!" It sounded like everyone was having fun. I'd soon be having fun with them.

I made it to the den and approached the bookshelf where I'd left the corsage. I patted the tops of the books and then the space behind them. My fingers found softness, like petals of skin.

"I'm back," Yun Sun said. The background sounds had diminished, suggesting she'd stepped outside. "And, Frankie, I know you're hurting. I *know* that. But what happened to Will was just a coincidence. A terrible, terrible coincidence."

"Call it what you want," I said. "I'm making my second wish." I plucked the corsage from behind the books.

Yun Sun's anxiety intensified. "Frankie, no, you can't!"

"Why not?"

"He fell from three hundred feet! His body was . . . they said he was mangled beyond . . . that's why they had a closed casket, remember?"

"So?"

"He's been rotting in a coffin for thirteen days!" she cried.

"Yun Sun, that is a tasteless thing to say. Honestly, if it were Jeremy being brought back to life, would we even be having this conversation?" I drew the flowers to my face, lightly touching the petals with my lips. "Listen, I've got to go. But save some punch for me! And Will! Ooo, make that *lots* of punch for Will—I bet he'll be absolutely crazed with thirst!"

I flipped my phone shut. I held the corsage aloft.

"I wish for Will to be alive again!" I cried exultantly.

The stench of decay thickened the air. The corsage curled, as if the petals were shrinking in on themselves. I flung it away on autopilot, just as I'd shake off an earwig that chanced to light on my hand. But whatever. The corsage wasn't important. What was important was Will. Where *was* he?

I glanced around, ridiculously expecting him to be sitting on the sofa, looking at me like *You're scared of a bunch of dried flowers? Pitiful!*

The sofa was empty, a gloomy, looming shape by the wall.

I darted to the window and peered out. Nothing. Just the wind, fluttering the leaves on the trees.

"Will?" I said.

Again nothing. A tremendous well of disappointment opened inside me, and I sank into my father's leather armchair.

Stupid Frankie. Stupid, foolish, pathetic me.

Time passed. Cicadas chirped.

Stupid cicadas.

And then, so faint, a thud. And then another. I straightened my spine.

Gravel popped on the road . . . or maybe the driveway? The thuds came closer. They were labored and with the odd offbeat of a limp, or of something being dragged.

I strained to hear.

There—a thump, ten feet away on the porch. A thump that was distinctly inhuman.

My throat closed as Yun Sun's words wormed back to me. *Mangled*, she'd said. *Rotting*. I wasn't paying attention before. Now it was too late. What had I done?

I jumped out of the chair and fled to the entry hall, safe from the eyes of anyone—or anything—who might choose to peer through the den's wide windows. What, exactly, had I brought back to life?

A knock echoed through the house. I whimpered, then clapped my hand over my mouth.

"Frankie?" a voice called. "I'm, uh . . . yikes. I'm kind of a mess." He laughed his self-deprecating laugh. "But I'm here. That's the important thing. I'm here to take you to prom!"

"We don't have to go to prom," I said. Was that *me* sounding so shrill? "Who needs prom? I mean, seriously!"

"Yeah, sure, this from the girl who would kill for the perfect romantic evening." The knob rattled. "Aren't you going to let me in?"

I hyperventilated.

There was a series of plops, like overripe strawberries being dropped into the trash, and then, "Aw, dude. Not good."

"Will?" I whispered.

"This is so uncool . . . but do you have any stain remover?"

Holy crap. Holy, holy, holy crap.

"You're not mad, are you?" Will asked. He sounded worried. "I came as fast as I could. But it was so frickin' *weird*, Frankie. Because, like . . ."

My mind flew to airless caskets, deep in the ground. *Please, no*, I thought.

"Forget it. It was weird—let's leave it at that." He tried to lighten things up. "Now are you going to let me in, or what? I'm falling to pieces out here!"

I pressed my body against the hall wall. My knees buckled, I wasn't doing too well with muscle control, but I reminded myself that I was safe behind the solid front door. Whatever else he was, Will was still flesh and bones. Well, partially. But not yet a ghost who could move through walls.

"Will, you've got to go," I said. "I made a mistake, okay?"

"A mistake? What do you mean?" His confusion broke my heart.

"It's just . . . oh God." I started crying. "We're not right for each other anymore. You understand, don't you?"

"No, I don't. You wanted me to ask you to prom, so I asked you to prom. And now for no good reason . . . *ohhh!* I get it!"

"You do?"

"You don't want me to see you! That's it, isn't it? You're nervous about how you look!"

"Um . . ." Should I run with this? Should I say yes just so he would leave?

"Frankie. Dude. You have nothing to worry about." He laughed. "One, you're beautiful; and two, compared to me, there's no way you won't look like . . . I don't know, an angel from heaven."

He sounded relieved, as if he'd had a niggling sense of something being off, but couldn't quite place his finger on it. But now he knew: It was Frankie having self-esteem issues, that's all! Silly Frankie!

I heard a shuffling, and then the bump of a small wooden lid. My body tensed, because I knew that bump.

The milk box—crap. He'd remembered the key in the milk box.

"I'm letting myself in," he called, slump-thumping back to the front door. "'Kay, Franks? 'Cause all of a sudden I'm, like, dying to see you!"

He laughed, jubilant. "I mean, wait, that came out wrong . . . but, heck, guess that's the theme of the night. *Everything's* coming out wrong—and I do mean everything!"

I fled to the den, where I got on my hands and knees and frantically patted the floor. If only it weren't so dark!

The deadbolt stuck, and Will jangled the key. His

breathing was clotted.

"I'm coming, Frankie!" he called. *Jangle, jangle.* "I'm coming as fast as I can!"

My fear ratcheted so high that I was thrown into an altered state of reality. I was gasping and crying out, I could hear myself, and my hands were blind feelers, pawing and slapping as I crawled.

With a thunk, the bolt slid home.

"*Yes,*" Will crowed.

The door swished over the frayed carpet at the exact instant my fingers closed on the crumbling corsage.

"Frankie? Why is it so dark? And why aren't you—"

I squeezed my eyes shut and spoke my final wish.

All sounds ceased, save for the rustle of wind in the leaves. The door, continuing its slow trajectory, bumped against the doorjamb. I stayed where I was on the floor. I sobbed, because my heart was breaking. No, my heart was broken.

After several moments, the cicadas once again took up their yearning chorus. I rose to my feet, stumbled across the room, and stood, shivering, in the open doorway. Outside, a pale shaft of moonlight shone on the deserted road.

Madison Avery
and the
Dim Reaper

KIM HARRISON

1

A BRITISH GENERAL, *a damsel in a dress, and a pirate walk into a gym,* I thought as I gazed over the bodies moving in a mind-numbing chaos of pent-up, inexperienced, teenage lust. Leave it to Covington High to turn prom into a joke. Not to mention my seventeenth birthday. What was I doing here? Prom was supposed to be real dresses with a live band, not rented costumes with canned music and streamers. And my birthday was supposed to be . . . anything but this.

"You sure you don't want to dance?" Josh yelled in my ear, sending his sugary breath over me. I tried not to grimace, keeping my gaze fixed on the clock beside the gym's scoreboard and wondering if an hour was long enough to stay and not get the third degree from my dad. The music was dull—the same rhythmic thump over, and over, and over. Nothing new in the last forty minutes. And the bass was way too loud.

"Yep," I said, edging away in time with the music when his hand tried to creep to my waist. "Still don't want to dance."

"Something to drink?" he tried again, and I cocked my hip, crossing my arms to hide my cleavage. I was still waiting for the boob fairy to show up, but the dress's corset shoved everything up and together to make it look like I had more than I did, making me self-conscious.

"No, thanks," I said with a sigh. He probably didn't hear me, but he got the gist, seeing as he looked away, watching everyone move. Long ballroom gowns and skimpy barmaid costumes mixed with swashbuckling pirates and sailors. That was the theme of the prom. Pirates. God! I had worked for two months on the prom committee at my old school. It was going to have been freaking fantastic, with a moonlit barge and a real band, but no-o-o-o. Mom had said Dad needed to spend time with me. That he was going through a midlife crisis and had to reconnect with something from his past that didn't involve arguing. I think she just got scared when she caught me sneaking out for a late cappuccino and shipped me back to Dad and Dullsville USA knowing I listened to him more than her. Okay, so it had been after midnight. And I might have been after more than caffeine. And yeah, I'd already been grounded from staying out too late the previous weekend, but that's why I had to sneak out.

Running the stiff lace of my colonial dress between my fingers, I wondered if any of these people had a clue what a real party looked like. Maybe they didn't care.

Josh was standing a little in front of me, bobbing his head in time with the music and clearly wanting to dance. Nearby at the food table was the guy who had skulked in after us. He was looking my way, and I gave him a stare, wondering if he was after me or Josh. Seeing my attention on him, the guy turned away.

My gaze fell back on Josh, who had begun to almost dance halfway between me and the moving people. Actually, I mused as he shifted and bobbed his head to the music, his costume made his thin, awkward height work for him—a traditional British general's red and white, complete with fake sword and epaulets. His father's idea, probably, since he was the VIP of VIPs at the research facility that had kept everyone employed when the military base moved to Arizona, but it did go with the overdone lace-and-corset thing I had on.

"Come on. Everyone else is dancing," he coaxed when he saw me look at him, and I shook my head, almost feeling sorry for him. He reminded me of the guys in the photography club pretending the darkroom door had locked to try to get a little action. It just wasn't

fair. I had spent three years learning how to fit in with
the cool chicks, and now I was right back with the nice
but unpopular guys, mowing down cupcakes in the
gym. And on my birthday, too.

"No," I said flatly. *Translation: Sorry, I'm not interested. You may as well give up.*

Even thick-headed, awkward, broken-glasses Josh
got that one, and he stopped his almost-dancing to fix
his blue eyes on me. "Jesus, you're a bitch, you know
that? I only asked you out because my dad made me. If
you want to dance, I'll be over there."

My breath caught, and I gaped at him as if he had
punched me in the gut. He cockily raised his eyebrows
and walked away with his hands in his pockets and his
chin raised. Two girls parted so he could walk between
them, and they hunched into each other in his wake,
gossiping as they glanced at me.

Oh my God. I'm a pity date. Blinking fast, I held my
breath as I fought to keep the room from going blurry.
Crap, not only was I the new girl, but I was a freaking
pity date! My dad had made nice to his boss, and he
made his son ask me out.

"Son of a dead puppy," I whispered, wondering if
everyone was looking at me or if it was just my imagination. I tucked my short blond hair behind my ear and
backed to the wall. Leaning against it with my arms
crossed, I tried to pretend Josh had gone to get some

pop. Inside, I was dying. I had been dumped. No, I had been dumped by a geek.

"Way to go, Madison," I said sourly, just imagining the gossip on Monday. I spotted Josh at the food table, pretending to ignore me without being obvious about it. The guy in the sailor outfit who had followed us in was talking to him. I still didn't think he was one of Josh's friends, even though he was jostling his elbow and pointing at the girls dancing in dresses cut too low for the gyrating they were doing. That I didn't recognize him wasn't surprising since I'd been avoiding everyone for the simple reason I wasn't happy being here and I didn't mind anyone knowing it.

I wasn't a jock or a nerd—though I had belonged to the photography club back home. Despite my efforts, I apparently didn't fit with the Barbie dolls. And I wasn't a goth, brain, druggie, or one of the kids who wanted to play scientist like their mommies or daddies at the research facility. I didn't fit anywhere.

Correction, I thought as Josh and the sailor laughed. *I fit with the bitches.*

The guy followed Josh's attention to another group of girls, who were now giggling at something Josh had said. His brown hair was frizzed out under his sailor's cap, and his crisp white outfit made him look like all the other guys who'd chosen sailor over pirate. He was tall, and there was a smooth grace to his movements that said he'd quit growing. He looked older than me, but he couldn't be too much older. It *was* the prom.

And I don't have to be here, I thought suddenly, shoving myself away from the wall with my elbows. Josh was my ride home, but my dad would pick me up if I called.

My motion to weave through the crowd to the double doors slowed in worry. He'd ask why Josh wasn't bringing me home. It would all come out. The lecture to be nice and fit in I could deal with, but the embarrassment . . .

Josh was watching me when I glanced up. The guy with him was trying to get his attention, but Josh's eyes were on mine. Mocking me.

That did it. No way was I going to call my dad. And I wasn't getting into a car with Josh, either. I'd walk it. All five miles. In heels. And a long cotton dress. On a damp April night. With my boobs scrunched together. What was the worst that could happen? A runaway cow incident? Crap, I really missed my car.

"Way to go, girl," I muttered, gathering my resolution along with my dress, head down as my shoulders bumped into dancers on my way to the door. I was so out of here. People were talking, but I didn't care. I didn't need friends. Friends were overrated.

The music melted into something fast, and I brought my attention up when the crowd seemed to shift, awkwardly changing rhythm. I jerked to a stop when I realized I was a step away from running into someone. "Sorry!" I shouted over the music, then froze, staring. *Holy crap, Mr. Sexy Pirate Captain. Where had he been the last three weeks, and were there more where he came from?*

I'd never seen him before. Not in the entire time I'd been stuck in this town. I would have remembered. Maybe exerted myself a little more. Flushing, I dropped my skirt to move my hand to cover my cleavage. God, I felt like a British tart with everything shoved up like that. The guy was dressed in a clingy black pirate costume, a pendant of gray stone lying on his chest. I could see it where the collar parted. A Zorro-style mask hid his upper face. The wide silk tails of it trailed down his back to mix with his luscious wavy black hair. He stood taller than me by about five inches, and as I ran my gaze over his tight figure, I wondered where he'd been keeping himself.

Certainly not the band room or Mrs. Fairel's U.S. Government class, I thought as the spinning lights played over him.

"My apologies," he said, taking my hand, and my breath caught, not because he was touching me, but because his accent wasn't Midwestern. Sort of a slow, soft exhalation laced with a crisp preciseness that told of taste and sophistication. I could almost hear the clink of crystal and soft laughter in it, the comforting sounds that more often than not had lulled me to sleep as the waves pushed on the beach.

"You aren't from around here," I blurted as I leaned to hear him better.

A smile grew, his dusky skin and dark hair almost a balm, so familiar amid the pale faces and light hair of the Midwestern prison I was in. "I'm here temporarily," he said. "An exchange student, in a manner of speaking. Same as you." He glanced disdainfully at the people moving around us with little rhythm and even less originality. "There are too many cows here, don't you think?"

I laughed, praying I didn't sound like a brainless flake. "Yes!" I almost shouted, pulling him down to talk into his ear over the noise. "But I'm not an exchange student. I moved here from Florida. My mom lives out there on the inner coastal, but now I'm stuck here with my dad. I agree. You're right, it's awful. At least you get to go home."

And where is home, Mr. Sexy Pirate?

A hint of low tide and canal water drifted to me, rising from him like a memory. And though some might find it unpleasant, tears pricked at my eyes. I missed my old school. I missed my car. I missed my friends. Why had Mom gone so ballistic?

"Home, yes," he said, and an intoxicating smile

showed a hint of tongue when he licked his lips and straightened. "We should leave the floor. We're in the way of their . . . dancing."

My heart pounded harder. I didn't want to move. He might go away, or worse, someone might slip their arm into his, claiming him. "Do you want to dance?" I said, nervous. "It's not what I'm used to, but it has a good beat."

His smile widened, and relief sent my pulse faster. *Oh God. I think he likes me.* Letting go of my hand, he nodded, and then dropped back a step and started to move.

For a moment, I forgot to follow and just watched him. He wasn't flamboyant. No, he went the other way— his slow movements making far more of an impact than if he had cleared the floor by spinning me around it.

Seeing me watching, he smiled from behind his mysterious mask and blue-gray eyes as he held out a hand for me to join him. I took a breath, my fingers slipping into his warm ones, and let him pull me into motion.

The music was the framework he moved within, and I lost myself trying to match the pattern of it. Almost swaying, we shifted at every second beat. I let myself relax and just dance, finding it easier if I didn't think about it. I could feel every shift of my hips and roll of my shoulders—and a thrill of something began to grow inside me.

While everyone around us continued with sharp, fast motions, we danced slow, the space between us narrowing, our gazes fixing more and more on each other as I became increasingly sure of myself. I let him guide me as the music pulsed and my heart pounded with it.

"Most everyone here calls me Seth," he said, almost ruining the moment, but then his hand curved lightly about my waist, and I leaned into him. *Oh yeah. This was better.*

"Madison," I said, liking how I felt, dancing slower than everyone else. But the music was fast, thumping to make my blood race. The two extremes made it seem all the more daring. "I haven't seen you around. Are you a senior?"

Seth's fingers tightened on the light cotton of my dress, or perhaps he was just drawing me closer. "I'm top of my class," he said, leaning so he wouldn't have to shout.

The colored lights played upon him, and I felt airy. Josh could suck an egg for all I cared. This was what my prom should be. "That would explain it," I said, tilting my head to see his eyes and try to place him. "I'm a junior."

He smiled with his lips closed, and I felt small and protected. My own smile grew. I could feel people starting to watch us, their dancing slowing as they turned. I hoped Josh was getting a good look. *Call me a bitch, would he?*

I lifted my chin, daring to reach out and pull Seth

near, our bodies touching, then moving apart. My heart hammered at what I was doing, but I wanted to hurt Josh. I wanted the gossip tomorrow to be what an idiot he had been to walk away from me. I wanted . . . something.

Seth's hands slid smoothly at my waist, neither imprisoning nor demanding, freeing me to dance as I wanted, and I let myself go, motions turning more sultry than these backwoods bumpkins had seen anywhere but on their TV. My lips twitched when I saw Josh and that sailor kid he'd been talking with all this time. Josh's face was white with anger, and I simpered back.

"You want him to know you aren't with him?" Seth said wistfully, and my gaze jerked to his. "He hurt you," Seth said, and his dark hand left tingles where it touched my chin. "You should show him what he lost."

The moment balanced, and though I knew it was spiteful, I found myself nodding.

Seth eased to a halt, pulling me into him with a smooth, unbroken gesture. He was going to kiss me. I knew it. It was in every motion he made. My pulse hammered, and I tilted my head up to meet his lips with my own, feeling my knees lock. Around us, people slowed to watch, some laughing, some envious. My eyes closed, and I shifted my weight so that we were still dancing as we kissed.

It was everything I wanted. Heat washed into me

where we touched, spilling down through me like layers, each flaring up as his touch grew closer. Never had I been kissed like this, and I couldn't breathe, afraid I'd ruin it. My hands were at his waist, and they held him tighter as he cupped my jaw, holding me as if I might break. He tasted like wood smoke. I wanted more—but boy, did I know better.

A low sound lifted from him, softer than distant thunder. His hands tightened, and adrenaline spiked through me. The kiss had shifted.

Alarmed, I jerked back, breathless but feeling bright-eyed and exhilarated. Seth's moody eyes were fixed on mine with a light amusement that I had pulled away.

"It's only a game," he said. "He's wiser, now. So are you. He's not worth pain."

I blinked as the lights spun madly and the music continued, loud and untouched by our kiss. Everything was different, but only I had changed. I tore my gaze from Seth, my hand still on his waist for balance. There were spots of color on Josh's cheeks, and he looked angry.

I raised my eyebrows at him. "Let's go," I said, linking my arm with Seth's. I didn't think anyone would show up to challenge my position. Not after that kiss.

Confident, I stepped forward with Seth beside me. A path opened, and I felt like a queen. Though the music thumped and blared, everyone watched us make our way unimpeded to the double doors with their brown-paper wrappings decorated to look like the oak doors of a castle.

Plebeians, I thought when Seth pushed open the door and the cooler air of the hallway hit me. The door closed behind us, and the music dulled. I slowed to a stop, low heels scuffing on the tile. There was a paper-cloth-covered table against the wall with a tired-looking woman checking tickets. Farther down the hall three kids loitered at the main door. The memory of our kiss rose back through me, making me suddenly nervous. *This guy was gorgeous. Why was he with me?*

"Thank you," I mumbled, glancing up and away, then warmed as I wondered if he might think I was talking about the kiss. "I mean, for getting me out of there with my pride intact," I added, flushing deeper.

"I saw what he did." Seth rocked us into motion down the hallway away from everyone and to the parking lot. "It was either that or you dumping punch on his clothes. And you . . ." He hesitated until I looked at him. "You want your revenge more subtle than that."

A sloppy grin came over me, but I couldn't help it. "You think?"

He inclined his head, acting far older than he should. "Do you have a ride home?"

I jerked to a stop, and he continued a step before turning, his blue-gray eyes wide in alarm. It was cool out here, and I told myself that was why I had a sudden chill.

"I'm . . . sorry," he said, blinking and holding himself still. "I didn't mean . . . I'll stay with you while you arrange for someone to come. You don't know me from Adam."

"No, it's not that," I rushed, embarrassed for my sudden mistrust. I glanced back at the woman by the gym door who was watching us with an idle interest. "I should call my dad, is all. Let him know what's going on."

Seth smiled, his white teeth showing strongly. "Of course."

I fumbled for the purse that this dress had come with. He moved away a few feet as I dug out my phone and fidgeted, trying to remember the house's number. There was no answer, and we both turned at the noise of the gym door opening. Josh came out, and my jaw tightened.

The answering machine picked up, and in a rush, I blurted, "Hi, Dad. It's Madison." *Duh.* "I'm getting a ride home with Seth . . ." I looked at him in question for a last name.

"Adamson," he said softly, his eyes behind his mask fixed on Josh. Damn, he had beautiful eyes. And long, luscious eyelashes.

"Seth Adamson," I said. "Josh turned out to be a jerk. I'll be home in a few minutes, okay?" But since no one was really there, there wasn't much my dad could say. I waited as if listening for a moment, then added, "I'm fi-i-i-ine. He was a jerk, is all. I'll see you in a minute."

Satisfied, I closed the phone and tucked it away, linking my arm through Seth's and turning us to the back doors as Josh caught up, his dress shoes clacking on the tile.

"Madison . . ." He was annoyed, and my satisfaction grew.

"Hi, Josh!" I said brightly, my tension rising as he fell into step on my other side. I didn't look at him, and I felt myself go hot. "I got a ride home. Thanks." *For nothing,* I added in my thoughts, still mad at him. Or my dad, maybe, for setting this up.

"Madison, wait."

He caught my elbow, and I spun to a halt. Josh froze, pulling back and letting go. "You're a jerk," I said, eyeing his costume and thinking it looked lame now. "And I'm no one's pity date. You can just . . . flip off," I adlibbed, not wanting Seth to think I swore like a sailor.

Reaching, Josh grabbed my wrist and yanked me away. "Listen to me," he said, and the fear in his eyes stopped my protest. "I've never seen this guy before. Don't be stupid. Let me take you home. You can tell your friends whatever you want. I'll go along with it."

I tried to take an insulted breath, but the corset wouldn't let me, so I lifted my chin instead. He knew I didn't have any friends. "I called my dad. I'll be fine," I said, glancing over his shoulder to the tall kid in that sailor outfit who had followed Josh out.

Still Josh wouldn't let go. Ticked, I twisted my arm, and when I reached to grab his wrist in a self-defense hold, he let go as if knowing it. Eyes wide, he backed up a step. "I'm going to follow you home then," he said, eyes flicking to Seth.

"Whatever," I said as I tossed my hair, secretly glad and wondering if maybe Josh wasn't so bad after all. "Seth, are you in the back lot?"

Seth came forward, a softly moving figure of grace and refinement next to Josh's commonality. "This way, Madison." I thought I saw a hint of victory in his eyes as his arm slipped through mine. No wonder. He'd obviously come to the prom by himself, and now Josh would be the one leaving alone.

I made sure my heels snapped smartly in a show of confident femininity as we went down the hall to the far set of doors. The dress made me feel elegant, and Seth looked fantastic. Josh and his silent buddy trailed behind like extras in a Hollywood film.

Seth held the door open for me, leaving the two guys to handle the swinging door by themselves. The air was chilly, and I wished I'd begged for an extra fifty from my dad to get the matching shawl for this outfit. I wondered if Seth would offer me his coat if I complained.

The moon was a hazy smear behind the clouds, and as Seth escorted me down the stairs, I could hear Josh behind me, talking softly to his friend in a low, derisive tone. My jaw clenched, and I followed Seth to a sleek black car parked illegally at the curb. It was a convertible, its top open to the cloudy skies, and I couldn't help but smile even wider. Maybe we could go for a drive before he took me home. Cold or not, I wanted to be seen in this car, sitting next to Seth, the wind in my hair and the music cranked. I bet he had great taste in music.

"Madison . . . ," Seth said in invitation, opening the door for me.

Feeling awkward and special all at the same time, I eased into the low front seat, my dress sliding on smooth leather. Seth waited while I got the rest of the skirt inside before gently shutting the door. I put on my belt as he crossed behind the car. The black paint glistened in the low glow of the security lights, and I ran my fingers over the smoothness, smug when I saw Josh jogging to his car.

Seth startled me when he slid in behind the wheel; I hadn't even heard the door open. He cranked the engine, and I liked the solid rumble of it. The stereo came on with something aggressive. The vocals weren't English, but that only added to it all. Josh's car's lights flashed on, and we pulled forward, Seth driving with one hand.

My pulse quickened as I looked at him across the dull light. The cool air felt thick against my skin, and as we picked up speed, the wind worked its way through my hair.

"I live to the south," I said when we reached the main road, and he turned the proper way. Josh's headlamps swung in behind us, and I settled myself in the seat, wishing Seth had offered me his coat. But he hadn't said a word or looked at me since I'd gotten in the car. Earlier, he'd been all sly confidence. Now it was . . . anticipation? And though I didn't know why, a slow feeling of alarm took root.

As if sensing it, Seth turned, driving the black road without looking. "Too late," he said softly, and I felt my face blank. "Easy. I told them it would be easy when you were young and stupid. Almost not worth the effort. Certainly not any enjoyment."

My mouth went dry. "Excuse me?"

Seth glanced at the road and back at me. The car started to go faster, and I gripped the door handle, pressing away from him. "Nothing personal, Madison. You're a name on a list. Or should I say, a soul to be culled. An important name, but a name nonetheless. They said it couldn't be done, and now, you'll be my admission to a higher court, you and your little life that will now not happen."

What the hell? "Josh," I said, turning to the lights going distant as Seth picked up speed. "He's following. My dad knows where I am."

Seth smiled, and I shivered at the moonlight glinting on his teeth. Everything else was lost in hazy moon shadow and the shriek of the wind. "Like that will make a difference?"

Oh my God. I was deep in it. My gut tightened. "Stop the car," I said forcefully, one hand on the door, the other holding my whipping hair out of my eyes. "Stop the car and let me out. You can't do this. People know where I am! Stop the car!"

"Stop the car?" he said, smirking. "I'll stop the car."

Seth shifted his leg, stomping on the brake and turning the wheel. I screamed, grabbing anything. The world spun. My breath left me in a shriek as the odd feeling of too much noise mixed with the cessation of jostling. We had left the road. Gravity pulled from the wrong way. Panic struck when I realized the car was flipping over.

Shit. I was in a convertible.

I ducked, hands clasped over the back of my neck, praying. A hard thump shook me and everything went black. My breath was crushed from me by the force of the hit. I think I was upside down. Then I was yanked another way. The sky brightened to gray, and I sucked in the air when the car flipped once more as it rolled down the embankment.

Again, the sky went black and the top of the car hit the ground. "No!" I shrieked, helpless, then groaned when the car slammed to a stop, upright. I was flung against the seat belt, agony stabbing through my back as I was thrown forward.

It was quiet. Breathing hurt. Oh God, I hurt all over, and I stared at the shattered windshield as I panted. The new edges of the window glinted dully in the moonlight, and I followed the broken line down the dash to find Seth gone. My insides hurt. I didn't see blood, but I think I broke something inside. *I was alive?*

"Madison!" came distant over my rasping breath. "Madison!"

It was Josh, and I forced my eyes up to the twin balls of light at the top of the embankment. A shadowy figure was sliding down. *Josh.*

I took a breath to call to him, groaning when someone took my head and turned me away.

"Seth?" I whispered. He looked untouched, standing outside the ruined car at my door in his costume of black pirate silk. The moon caught his eyes and pendant, giving them both a gray sheen.

"Still alive," he said flatly, and tears started to slip from me. I couldn't move, but everything was a massive ache so I didn't think I was paralyzed. Damn it, this was a sucky birthday. Dad was going to kill me.

"I hurt," I said, my voice small, then thought, *What a stupid thing to say.*

"I don't have time for this," Seth said, clearly bothered.

My eyes widened, but I didn't move when he pulled from the folds of his costume a short blade. I tried to cry out, but my breath left me when he pulled his arm back as if to strike me. Moonlight glinted on the blade, red with someone else's blood. *Fantabulous. He's a psycho. I left the prom with a knife-wielding psycho. Can I pick 'em, or what?*

"No!" I shrieked, managing to get my arms up, but the blade was a whisper of ice passing through me, leaving me unhurt. I stared at my middle, not believing I was uncut. My dress wasn't torn and blood wasn't flowing, but I knew that blade had gone through me. It had gone through me and the car both.

Not understanding, I gaped up at Seth, now standing with the blade at rest and watching me. "What . . . ," I tried to say when I realized nothing hurt anymore. But my voice was utterly absent. He arched his eyebrows in a show of scorn. My expression left me when I felt the first brush of utter nothing, both new and familiar, like a memory long lost.

The terrifying absence of everything crept through me, stilling each thought it rolled over. Soft and muzzy, a blanket of nothing started at the edges of my world and moved inward, taking first the moon, then the night, then my body, and finally the car. Josh's cries were swallowed up in a low hush of a thrum, leaving only Seth's silver eyes.

And then Seth turned and walked away.

"Madison!" I heard faintly, followed by the briefest touch on my cheek. Then even that melted and there was nothing.

2

THE MIST OF NOTHING slipped slowly from me in a painful series of prickles and the sound of two people arguing. I felt sick, not from my entire back tingling so painfully I could hardly stand to breathe, but from the feeling of helpless fear that the hushed, back-and-forth voices pulled from my past. I could almost smell the moldy fluff of my stuffed rabbit as I had curled into a ball and listened to the two people who were my entire world frighten me beyond belief. That they had both told me it hadn't been my fault hadn't lessened my grief at all. Grief I had to hold inside until it became a part of me. Pain that adhered to my bones. To cry in my mother's arms would say I loved her more. To cry into my dad's shoulder would say I loved him best. It was a crappy way to grow up.

But this . . . this wasn't my parents arguing. It sounded like two kids.

I took a breath to find it came easier. The last of the haze started to fade with the tingles, and my lungs moved, aching as if someone were sitting on them. Realizing my eyes were shut, I opened them to find a blurry black just before my nose. There was a heavy, pla-sticky smell.

"She was sixteen when she got in that car. It's your fault," a young but masculine voice said hotly, oddly muffled. I was getting the distinct impression that the argument had been going on for some time, but I only remembered snatches of it amid uneasy thoughts of nothing.

"You are *not* going to put this on me," a girl said, her voice just as hushed and determined. "She was seventeen when he flipped her coin. This is your screwup, not mine. God save you, she was right in front of you! How could you miss it?"

"I missed it because she wasn't seventeen!" he shot back. "She was sixteen when he picked her up. How was I supposed to know he was after her? How come you weren't there? You slipped up big time."

The girl gasped in affront. I was cold. Taking a deeper breath, I felt a surge of strength. Fewer tingles, more aches. It was stuffy, my breath coming back warm to me. It wasn't dark; I was in something.

"You little piss-ant!" the girl snapped. "Don't tell me I slipped up. She died at seventeen. That's why I wasn't there. I was never notified."

"But I don't do sixteen," he said, his voice going nasty. "I thought he was flipping the boy."

I suddenly realized the black blur throwing back my breath was a sheet of plastic. My hands came up, and my nails pushed through it in a stab of fear. Almost panicking, I sat up.

I'm on a table? It sure felt hard enough for one. I shoved the plastic off me. Two kids were standing by a set of dirty white swinging doors, and they spun in surprise. The girl's pale face went red, and the guy backed up as if embarrassed to have been caught arguing with her.

"Oh!" the girl said, tossing her long dark braid behind her. "You're up. Uh, hi. I'm Lucy, and this is Barnabas."

The guy dropped his eyes and waved sheepishly. "Hey," he said. "How you doing?"

"You were with Josh," I said, my finger shaking as I pointed, and he nodded, still not looking at me. His costume looked odd next to her shorts and tank top. Both of them wore a black stone pendant around their necks. They were dull and insignificant, but my eye went to them because they were the only thing the two shared. Other than their anger at each other and their surprise at me.

"Where am I?" I said, and Barnabas winced, a tall

form scuffing his feet against the tile. "Where's Josh?" I hesitated, realizing I was in a hospital, but . . . *Wait a minute. I was in a freaking body bag?* "I'm in the morgue?" I blurted. "What am I doing in the morgue?"

Moving wildly, I got my legs out of the plastic bag and slid to the floor, heels clicking in some weird counterpoint as I caught my balance. There was a tag on a rubber band around my wrist, and I yanked it off, taking some hair along with it. I had a long rip in my skirt, and heavy grease marked it. Dirt and grass were plastered to me, and I stank of field and antiseptic. So much for getting my deposit back.

"Someone made a mistake," I said as I shoved the tag in a pocket, and Lucy snorted.

"Barnabas," she said, and he stiffened.

"This is not my fault!" he exclaimed, rounding on her. "She was sixteen when she got in that car. I don't do sixteen! How was I supposed to know it was her birthday?"

"Yeah? Well, she was seventeen when she died, so it *is* your problem!"

Dead? Were they blind? "You know what?" I said, feeling more steady the longer I stood here. "You two can argue till the sun goes nova, but I have to find someone and tell them I'm okay." Heels clicking, I headed for the dirty white twin doors.

"Madison, wait," the guy said. "You can't."

"Watch me," I said. "My dad is going to be so-o-o-o ticked."

I strode past them, getting twenty feet before a feeling of disconnection hit me. Dizzy, I put a hand to an empty table as the odd sensation roared from nowhere. My hand cramped where it rested, and I pulled it away as if burned when it seemed the coldness of metal had touched my bone. I felt . . . spongy. Thin. The soft hum of the ventilation grew muffled. Even the pounding of my heart became distant. I turned, hand to my chest to try and make it feel normal again. "What . . ."

From across the room, Barnabas shrugged his thin shoulders. "You're dead, Madison. Sorry. You get too far from our amulets, and you start to lose substance."

He gestured to the gurney, and I looked.

My breath slammed out of me. Knees buckling, I half fell against the empty table. I was still there. I mean, I was still on the gurney. I was lying on the cart in a torn body bag, looking far too small and pale, my elaborate dress bunched up around me in an elegant display of forgotten grace out of time.

I was dead? But I could feel my heart beat.

Limbs going weak, I started to crumple.

"Swell. She's a fainter," the girl said dryly.

Barnabas lurched forward to catch me. His arms slid around me and my head lolled. At his touch, everything rushed back: sounds, smells, and even my pulse. My lids fluttered. Inches from me, Barnabas's lips pressed tight. He was so close, and I thought I could smell sunflowers.

"Why don't you shut up?" he said to Lucy as he eased me to the floor. "Show a little compassion? That's your job, you know."

The cold from the tile soaked into me, seeming to clear the gray about my sight. *How could I be dead? Did the dead pass out?* "I'm not dead," I said unsteadily, and Barnabas helped me sit up and put my back to a table leg.

"Yes, you are." He crouched beside me, his brown eyes wide and concerned. Sincere. "I'm really sorry. I thought he was going to flip Josh. They usually don't leave evidence like a car behind like that. You must really be a broken feather in their wing."

My thoughts flashed to the crash, and I put a hand to my stomach. Josh had been there. I remember that. "He thinks I'm dead. Josh, I mean."

From across the room came Lucy's caustic "You are dead."

I sent my gaze to the gurney, and Barnabas shifted to block my view. "Who are you?" I asked as the dizziness slipped away.

Barnabas stood. "We, ah, are Reconnaissance Error Acquisitions Personnel. Evaluation and Recovery."

I thought about that. Reconnaissance Error Acquisitions . . . *R.E.A.P.E.R.?*

Holy crap! A surge of adrenaline shot through me. I

scrambled up, eyes fixed on me on the gurney. I was here. I was alive! That might be me, but I was standing here, too. "You're grim reapers!" I exclaimed, feeling my way around the table and putting it between us. My toes started to go numb, and I stopped, my gaze darting to the amulet around Barnabas's neck. "Oh my God, I'm dead," I whispered. "I can't be dead. I'm not ready to be dead. I'm not done yet! I'm only seventeen!"

"We're *not* grim reapers." Lucy had her arms crossed defensively as if it were a sore spot. "We're white reapers. Black reapers kill people before their coin should be flipped, white reapers try to save them, and grim reapers are treacherous betrayers who brag too much and won't survive to see the sun turn back to dust."

Barnabas looked embarrassed as he shuffled his feet. "Grim reapers are white reapers who were tricked into working for . . . the other side. They don't do much culling since black reapers don't let them, but if there is a sudden, massive death toll, you know they'll show to pull a few souls early, in as dramatic a way as possible. They're hacks. No class at all."

This last was said with a bitter voice, and I wondered at the rivalry, backing up until I started going spongy again. Eyeing their amulets, I edged forward until the feeling went away. "You kill people. That's what Seth said. He said something about culling my soul! You *do* kill people!"

Barnabas ran a hand across the back of his neck. "Ah, we don't. Most of the time." He glanced at Lucy. "Seth is a black reaper, a dark reaper. We only show up when they target someone out of time, or there's been a mistake."

"Mistake?" My head swung up in hope. Did that mean they could put me back?

Lucy came forward. "You weren't supposed to die, see. A dark reaper took you out before your coin should have been flipped. It's our job to stop them, but we can't sometimes. We're here to make a formal apology and get you where you're going." Frowning, she looked at Barnabas. "And as soon as he admits it was his fault, I can get out of here."

I stiffened, refusing to look at me on the gurney. "I'm not going anywhere. If you made a mistake, fine. Just put me back! I'm right there." I took a step forward, scared out of my mind. "You can, right?"

Barnabas winced. "It's kinda too late. Everyone knows you're dead."

"I don't care!" I shouted. Then my face went cold in a sudden thought. Dad. He thought I was . . . "Dad . . . ," I whispered, panicking. Taking a breath, I turned to the swinging doors and broke into a run.

"Wait! Madison!" Barnabas shouted, but I hit the doors hard, stumbling through them even though they only swung three inches. But I was in the next room. I had sort of passed through them. As if I weren't even there.

There was a fat guy at a desk, and he looked up at the tiny squeak the doors made shifting. His little piggy eyes widened, and he took a huge breath. Mouth open, he pointed.

"There's been a mistake," I blurted, heading to the open archway and the dimly lit hall. "I'm not dead."

But I was feeling really weird again. Misty and thin. Stretched. Nothing sounded right, either, and the gray was edging my sight to make a tunnel-like vision.

Behind me, Barnabas pushed through the doors. Immediately the world shifted to normal. It *was* the amulet he wore that kept me solid. I had to get me one of those.

"Yes, she is," he said, never slowing down until he grabbed my wrist. "You're hallucinating. She's not really here. Neither am I."

"Where did you come from?" the guy managed, staring. "How did you get in there?"

Lucy shoved in, the swinging door banging against the wall to make me and Desk Guy jump. "Madison, quit being a stiff. You gotta go."

This was too much for the technician, and he reached for the phone.

I twisted my wrist, but Barnabas wouldn't release me. "I have to talk to my dad!" I exclaimed, and he yanked me off balance.

"We're leaving," he said, a new threat in his eyes. "Right now."

Frantic, I stomped on his foot. Barnabas howled, his gangly form bending double as he let go. Lucy laughed at him, and I darted for the hallway. *Try to stop me*, I thought, then ran right into something big, warm, and smelling of silk. I backed up, becoming scared when I saw it was Seth. He had killed me with a sword that left no mark when driving me off a cliff failed to do it. He was a dark reaper. He was my death.

"Why are there two of you?" he asked as he looked at Barnabas and Lucy. The cadence of his voice was familiar, but the sound of it hit my ears wrong. And the scent of sea now smelled like rot. "That's right," he added, pulling his gaze back to me, and I shuddered. "You died on the anniversary of your birth. Two reapers. My, my, my. Such the drama queen, Madison. I'm glad you're up. It's time to go."

Hunched and afraid, I retreated. "Don't touch me."

"Madison!" Barnabas shouted. "Run!"

But there was only the morgue to run to. Lucy got in front of me, hands spread wide as if she could stop Seth with her will alone. "What are you doing here?" she said, voice shaking. "She's already dead. You can't flip her twice."

Seth scuffed his shoes confidently. "As you said, I flipped her coin. She's mine if I want her."

Barnabas paled. "You never come back for them.

You're . . ." His eyes darted to the stone about Seth's neck. "You're not a black reaper, are you?"

Seth grinned as if it was a big joke. "No. I'm not. I'm a little bit more. More than you can handle. Leave, Barnabas. Just walk away. It won't hurt if you do."

I stared at Barnabas, helpless. His brown eyes met mine, saw my fear. I watched him visibly gather his courage.

"Barnabas!" Lucy shouted, terrified. "Don't!"

But Barnabas launched himself at the dark figure in black silk. In a motion so casual it was frightening, Seth turned to smack him with the back of his hand. Arms and legs flailing, Barnabas flew backward, hitting the wall and slumping to the floor, out cold.

"Run!" Lucy shouted, pushing me toward the morgue. "Stay in the sun. Don't let the black wings touch you. We'll get help. Someone will find you. Get out of here!"

"How?" I exclaimed. "He's in front of the only door."

Seth moved again, this time backhanding Lucy. She crumpled where she stood, leaving only me since the technician had either passed out or was hiding under the desk. Jaw trembling, I stood to my full height—such as it was—and tugged my dress straight. *Deeper in it yet, apparently.*

"She meant," Seth said, his voice both familiar and strange, "to run through the walls. You had a better chance against the black wings in the sun than with me under the ground."

"But I can't . . . ," I started, then looked at the swinging doors. I went through them, having shifted them open only a few inches. What the heck was I? A ghost?

Seth smiled, chilling me. "Nice to see you, Madison, now that I can really . . . see you." He took off his mask and let it drop. His face was beautiful, like chiseled stone made soft.

I licked my lips and went cold to the bone when I remembered him kissing me. Holding one arm to myself, I backed away, trying to get out of Barnabas's and Lucy's influence so I could run through the walls. Hey, if Mr. Creepy thought I could do it, then maybe I could.

Seth followed, step for step. "We leave together. No one will believe I culled you unless I throw you at their feet."

Heels clicking, I kept moving. My gaze darted to Barnabas and Lucy, both still sprawled on the tile. "I'd rather stay, thanks." My heart pounded, and my back hit the wall. A little yelp slipped from me. I was far enough away from them that I should be misty, but I wasn't. I stared at Seth, then at that black stone about his neck. It was the same. *Damn it!*

"You don't have a choice," he said. "I'm the one that killed you. You're mine."

He reached out, grabbing my wrist. Adrenaline surged, and I twisted.

"The hell I am," I said, then kicked him in the shins. He clearly felt it, grunting as he bent in pain, but didn't let go. He had put his face in my reach, though, and grabbing his hair, I slammed his nose against my rising knee. I felt cartilage snap, and my stomach turned.

Cursing in a language that hurt my head, he let go and fell back.

I had to get out of here. I had to be solid or I'd never make it. Heart pounding, I grabbed the stone about his neck, pulling the necklace over his ears and off him. It tingled in my hand like fire, and I clenched my fingers around it, willing to suffer if it meant I would be whole.

Seth hit the floor, gaping up at me with red blood covering his face. He looked as surprised as if he had run into a glass wall.

"Madison . . . ," Barnabas rasped from the floor.

I turned, seeing him stare at me with pain-laced, unfocused eyes.

"Run," he gasped.

Seth's amulet in my hand, I turned to the open hallway . . . and I ran.

3

"D**AD!**" I STOOD IN the open front door, heart pounding as I listened to the silence seep up from the tidy, well-ordered state my dad kept the house in. Behind me, a lawn mower droned in the early sun. The gold haze spilled in to glint on the hardwood floors and the banister leading upstairs. I had run the entire way in my heels and that obnoxious dress. People had stared, and that I wasn't a bit tired kind of freaked me out. My pulse was fast from fear, not exertion.

"Dad?"

I stepped in, my eyes pricking with emotion when from upstairs came my dad's incredulous, shaky voice calling, "Madison?"

I took the stairs two at a time, tripping on my skirt and clawing my way up the last step. Throat tight, I rustled to a stop in the doorway to my room. My dad was sitting on the floor amid my boxes, opened but never unpacked. He looked old, his thin face gaunt with heartache, and I couldn't move. I didn't know what to do.

Eyes wide, he stared as if I weren't there. "You never unpacked," he whispered.

A hot tear ran down to my chin, coming from nowhere. Seeing him like this, I realized he did need me to remind him of the good stuff. No one had ever needed me before. "I . . . I'm sorry, Dad . . . ," I managed as I stood there, helpless.

He took a breath and snapped out of it. Emotion lit his face. In a surge of motion, he stood. "You're alive?" he breathed, and I gasped when he took the three steps between us and brought me to him in a crushing hold. "They said you were dead. You're alive?"

"I'm okay," I sobbed into his chest, the release washing through me so hard it was painful. He smelled like the lab he worked in, of oil and ink, and nothing ever smelled so good. I couldn't stop my tears. I was dead—I think. I had an amulet, but I didn't know if I was going to be able to stay, and the fear of that fed my helplessness. "I'm okay," I said around a hiccupping sob. "But there was a mistake."

Half laughing, he pushed me back enough to see my face. Tears brightened his eyes, and he smiled as if he'd never stop. "I was at the hospital," he said. "I saw you."

The memory of that pain crossed behind his eyes, and he touched my hair with a shaking hand as if to reassure himself I was real. "But you're okay. I tried to call your mother. She's going to think I'm crazy. More crazy than usual. I couldn't leave a message telling her you were in an accident. So I hung up. But you're really okay?"

My throat was tight, and I sniffed loudly. *I was not going to give up my amulet. Never.* "I'm sorry, Dad," I said, still crying. "I shouldn't have gone with that guy. I never should have. I'm sorry. I'm so sorry!"

"Shhhh." He pulled me back into a hug, rocking me, but I only cried harder. "It's okay. You're all right," he soothed, his hand brushing my hair. But he didn't know I really was dead.

His breath catching, my dad halted in a sudden thought. He put me at arm's length, and the cold that spilled into me when he looked me over ended my tears in a soft sniffle. "You're really fine," he said in wonder. "Not a scratch on you."

I smiled nervously, and one of his arms slipped from me. "Dad, there's something I need to tell you. I—"

There was a soft scuff at the door. My dad's eyes shot over my shoulder, and I turned to find Barnabas standing awkwardly next to a short man in a loose, martial arts kind of an outfit. It was billowy. Not functional at all. He was upright and thin, with sharp features and very dark skin. His eyes were a deep brown, heavily lined at the corners. His hair, too, said he was old, the tight curls graying at the temples.

"I'm sorry," my dad said, pulling me to stand beside him. "Did you bring my daughter home? Thank you."

I didn't like Barnabas's grimace, and I had to work to not hide behind my dad. His arm was still around me, and I didn't want to move. Crap. I think Barnabas had brought his boss. I wanted to stay. *Damn it, I don't want to be dead. This isn't fair!*

The dark man made a rueful face. "No," he said, the word having a pleasant crispness. "She managed that all by herself. God knows how."

I wiped my eyes, frightened. "They didn't bring me home," I said, shifting nervously. "I don't know them. I've seen the guy," I added, "but not the old man."

Still, my dad smiled neutrally, trying to piece it together. "Are you from the hospital?" he asked, and then his face hardened. "Who's responsible for telling me my daughter was dead? Someone's head is going to roll over this."

Barnabas cringed, and his boss sniffed his agreement. "Truer words have not been said, sir." His eyes traveled over my room, taking in the pink walls, white furniture, and opened boxes never fully unpacked. They landed on me last, and I wondered what conclusions he'd made. With my life ending so abruptly, I was sort of like my room—everything was here, but nothing out of the boxes. And now everything would get taped back shut and shoved into a closet, all the good stuff never seen or realized. *I'm not done yet.*

I stiffened when the man took a step into my room, a thin hand raised placatingly. "We need to talk, child," he said, striking me cold.

Oh God. He wanted me to go with him.

I clutched the amulet to me, and my dad's grip on me tightened. He saw my frightened eyes and finally understood something was wrong. Shifting, he put himself between me and the two people in the doorway. "Madison, call the police," he said, and I reached for the phone on the bedside table. *That* I had unpacked.

"Ah, we need a moment," the old man said.

I pulled my attention up as he waved his hand like a bad actor in a science fiction movie. The hum of the open line cut off, and from outside, the mower quit. Shocked, I stared at the phone, then my dad standing between me and the two men. He wasn't moving.

My knees felt watery. Setting the phone back in the cradle, I stared at my dad. He seemed all right. Apart from the not-moving thing.

The old man sighed, and my attention jerked to him. *Son of a dead puppy,* I thought, cold and scared. I wasn't leaving without a fight.

"Let him go," I said, my voice trembling. "Or I'll . . . I'll . . ."

Barnabas's lips quirked, and the man arched his eyebrows. His eyes were a grayish blue. I could have sworn they had been brown. "You'll what?" he said, taking a firmer stance on the carpet with his arms over his chest.

I glanced at my dad, frozen. "I'll scream, or something," I threatened.

"Go ahead. No one will hear you. It will be a pop of nothing, too fast to be heard."

I took a breath to chance it, and he shook his head. My breath exploded out of me and I backpedaled when he lurched into the room. But he wasn't coming for me. Yanking my white chair from the vanity, he sat with his small body at an angle. He dropped an elbow onto the top and then cradled his forehead in his hand as if weary. He made an odd picture against the music box and girl stuff.

"Why can't anything be easy?" he muttered, fingering my ceramic zebras. "Is this a joke?" he said louder at the ceiling. "Are you laughing? Getting a good laugh out of this, are you?"

I looked at the door, and Barnabas shook his head in warning. Fine. There was still the window—though with this dress, I might kill myself if I fell. Oh, wait. I was dead already. "Is my dad okay?" I asked, daring to touch his elbow.

Barnabas nodded, and the old man brought his gaze back to me. Grimacing as if making a decision, he extended his hand. I stared at it, not reaching for it. "Pleasure to make your acquaintance," he said firmly. "Madison, was it? Everyone calls me Ron."

I stared at him, and he slowly put his arm down. His eyes were brown again. "Barnabas told me what you did," he said. "Can I see it?"

Surprised, I fidgeted, my fingers sliding off my dad's arm. Man . . . this was creepy. It was like the entire world had stopped, but I was a walking dead, so I guess my dad being frozen was a small thing. "See what?"

"The stone," Ron said, and the hint of anxiety in his voice struck me like fire.

He wanted it. He wanted it, and it was the only thing keeping me alive. Or not quite dead. "I don't think so," I said, sure of its value when Ron's expression became alarmed as my hand crept up to feel the stone's cool surface.

"Madison," he soothed, standing. "I simply want to look at it."

"You want it!" I exclaimed, heart pounding. "It's the only thing keeping me solid. I don't want to die. You guys messed up. I'm not supposed to be dead! It's your fault!"

"Yes, but you *are* dead," Ron said, and my breath hissed in when he extended his hand. "Just let me look at it."

"I'm not giving it up!" I shouted, and Ron's eyes lit in fear.

"Madison, no! Don't say it!" he shouted, reaching.

I stumbled back out of my dad's questionable protection, clutching it. "It's mine!" I shrieked, my back hitting the wall.

Ron lurched to a halt, dismay clear on his old features as his arm dropped. The world seemed to balance. "Oh, Madison," he breathed. "You really shouldn't have."

Not knowing why he had stopped, I stared at him, then stiffened when a shiver moved through me. A cramping-ice feeling rose from my palm and the amulet, and it raced through my entire body, making me stiffen. It was like an electrical shock. I heard my pulse echo in me, the thump coming back from the inside of my skin before it filled the space and made me feel almost . . . whole. An instant later, it backlashed with a feeling of heat to balance out the cold, and then . . . it was done.

My breath slammed out of me, and I stood, frozen with my back to the wall. Heart pounding, I stared at Ron. He had a miserable look, quiet and depressed in his robes. I was afraid to move. But the amulet in my hand felt different. Little sparkles of sensation still shot from it, and unable to stop myself, I opened my fingers to look. My jaw dropped, and I stared. It wasn't the same. "Look!" I said stupidly. "It changed."

His back bowed, Ron slumped into the chair, muttering under his breath. Shocked, I dropped the pendant to hold it by the cord. When I had ripped it from the black reaper, it had been a simple, gray, river-washed stone. Now it was utterly black, like a spot of nothing dangling from the cord. The black wire cradling it had taken on a silver sheen, catching the light and throwing it around the room. *Crap. Maybe I had broken it.* But it was beautiful. How could it be broken?

"That's not what it looked like when I got it," I said, then went cold at the look of pity Ron now wore. Behind him, Barnabas looked almost terrified, his face white and his eyes wide.

"You got that right," Ron said bitterly. "We had a hope of ending this properly until you claimed it. But no-o-o, now it's yours." His eyes met mine in wry disgust. "Congratulations."

Slowly my hand dropped, and I shifted nervously. It was mine. He said it was mine.

"But it was a black reaper's stone," Barnabas said, and I started at the fear in his voice. "That thing wasn't a reaper, but it had a reaper's stone. She's a black reaper!"

My lips parted. "Whoa, wait up."

"She's a black reaper!" Barnabas shouted, and my jaw dropped when he shook his shirt and brought out a short hand scythe, twin to Seth's. Jumping, he got between me and Ron.

"Barnabas!" Ron bellowed, cuffing him to send him stumbling back to the door. "She's not a black reaper, you idiot! She's not even a white one. She can't be. She's human, even if she is dead. Put that away before I age it to rust!"

"But it's a black reaper's stone," he stuttered, his narrow shoulders hunched. "I saw her take it!"

"And whose fault is it that she knew what it was, Barney?" he mocked, and the young man dropped back, ducking his head, clearly embarrassed.

My heart pounded as I stood in the corner, holding the pendant so tight my fingers hurt. Ron glanced disparagingly between us. "That isn't a black reaper's stone any more than a black reaper would be strong enough to leave corporal evidence of its existence behind, or . . . ," he continued, raising a hand to keep Barnabas from interrupting, "have a reason to come back for the soul of someone they culled. She's got something more powerful than a reaper stone, and they'll be back for it. You can count on it."

Oh great. Just swell.

Barnabas seemed to draw himself back together, looking worried and scared. "He said he wasn't a reaper, but I thought he was trying to cow us. What is he if he isn't a reaper?"

"I don't know yet. But I have a few ideas."

Ron's admission of ignorance was worse than anything he could have said, and a ribbon of fear pulled through me. I shuddered, and Ron sighed when he saw it. "I should been watching for this," he murmured. Then looking at the heavens, he bellowed, "A memo would have been nice!"

His voice echoed, accentuating the muffled nothing that gripped the world. Remembering these two people weren't really people, I looked at my dad, as frozen and unmoving as a mannequin. They wouldn't hurt him, would they? To cover up their mistake with me?

"Dust to stars," Ron said softly. "We'll simply adapt the best we can."

The older man stood with a heavy sigh. Seeing him moving, I pushed from the corner to get between him and my dad. Ron looked at my raised hand as if I were a kitten holding off a dog who stopped only because he wasn't interested.

"I'm not leaving," I said, standing in front of my dad as if I could actually do something. "And you aren't going to touch my dad. I have a stone. I'm solid. I'm alive!"

Ron looked me in the eye. "You have a stone, but you don't know how to use it. And you aren't alive. This delusion of pretending to be is a bad idea. However, seeing as you have a stone, and *they* have your body—"

My gaze darted to Barnabas, seeing by his uncomfortable expression that it was true. "Seth? He has my body?" I said, suddenly afraid. "Why?"

Ron reached out, and I jumped as his hand landed

on my shoulder. It was warm, and I could feel his support—not that I thought he could really do anything to help me. "To keep you from crossing over and thereby able to give us the stone permanently?" he guessed, his dark eyes filled with pity. "As long as they have your body, you're stuck here. That stone you took is clearly an important one. It shifted to adapt to your mortal abilities. Very few stones can do that. Usually when a human claims a stone, it simply atomizes them in a surge of overload."

My mouth dropped open, and Ron nodded sagely. "Claiming the divine when one is not is a sure way to blow your soul to dust."

I closed my mouth, stifling a shiver.

"If we have it," Ron continued, "they're potentially at a disadvantage. It's in limbo right now, like you—a coin spinning on edge."

His hand slipped away. I felt all the more alone and small, though I stood taller than him.

"As long as you remain on the corporal side of things, they have a hope of finding you," he said, moving to look out my window at a world that had slowed to almost no movement.

"But Seth knows where I am," I said, confused, and Ron spun slowly around.

"Physically, yes, but he left here rather abruptly with your body. He crossed without a stone to make a memory of exactly where you are in time. It will be hard to find you again. Especially if you don't do anything to draw attention to yourself."

Miss Anonymity. Yeah, I can do that. Ri-i-i-i-ight. My head hurt, and I held one arm to me with the other and tried to make sense of what he was telling me.

"He will find you, though. Find you and take you and that stone back with him. What happens then?" Shaking his head, he turned to the window again, the light spilling in to outline him in gold. "They do terrible things, without thought, to further themselves."

Seth had my body. I felt myself go pale. Barnabas saw it, then cleared his throat to get Ron's attention. The old man's eyes landed on me, and he blinked as if realizing what he had said. "Ah, I could be wrong," he said, not helping. "I am, sometimes."

My pulse quickened, and I felt a jolt of panic. Before the accident Seth had said I was his ticket to a higher court. He didn't just want me dead. He wanted me. Not the stone I stole from him. Me. I opened my mouth to tell Ron, then, frightened, changed my mind. Barnabas saw in my sudden fear that I was withholding something, but Ron was moving, crossing my room with sharp steps and shooing him out. Barnabas silently retreated to the hall, his mouth shut and his head down in thought, probably afraid that whatever I wasn't saying would get him in more trouble, not less. Alarm trickled through me. They weren't leaving, were they?

"The only thing we can do now," Ron said, "is keep you intact until we find out how to break the hold the stone has on you without breaking your soul."

"But you just said I can't die," I said. *Just where did he think he was going? Seth was going to be back!*

Ron stopped at the threshold. Barnabas stood behind him, a worry too deep for a mere seventeen years showing heavy on him. "You can't die because you're already dead," the old man said. "But there are worse things."

Great, I thought, warming when I recalled dancing with Seth, that kiss he took, the feel of his nose breaking against my knee, and the look of hatred he had given me. *Way to go, Madison.* Not only did I screw up my reputation at a new school, but I managed to insult the angel of death, too. Put myself at the top of his wish list.

"Barnabas?" Ron said, making me jump. Barnabas, too, looked surprised.

"Sir?"

"Congratulations, you've been promoted to guardian angel."

Barnabas froze, then looked aghast at me. "That's not a promotion. It's a punishment!"

"Some of this is your fault," Ron said, his voice harsh in comparison to the sly smile he gave me, but Barnabas couldn't see it. "Most, probably." His face went serious. "Deal with it. And don't take it out on her."

"But Lucy. It was her responsibility!" he protested, looking young as he whined.

"Madison is seventeen," Ron said, his tone brooking no argument. "You handle seventeen. Should be a snap." He turned, hands on his hips. "In addition to your regular white-reaper prevention detail, you will be Madison's guardian angel. I'd think we could get this sorted out in a year." His gaze went distant. "One way or another."

"But sir!" he exclaimed, stumbling into the hall's wall when Ron pushed past him to the stairs. I followed, not believing this. *I have a guardian angel?*

"Sir, I can't!" Barnabas said, making me feel like an unwelcome burden. "I can't do my job *and* watch her! If I get too far away, they'll take her!"

"Then keep her with you when you work." Ron went several steps down. "She needs to learn how to use that thing. Teach her something in your *copious* spare time. Besides, it's not like you have to keep her alive. Just keep her coin spinning. Try to do a better job of it this time," he almost growled.

Barnabas sputtered, and Ron turned to smile worriedly at me. "Madison," he said in farewell. "Keep the pendant with you. It will protect you somewhat. If you take it off, black wings can find you, and the dark reapers are never far from them."

Black wings. There was that phrase again. Just the name invoked a nasty image in my thoughts. "Black wings?" I asked, the two words sounding completely foul on my lips.

Ron paused on the first step. "Filthy vultures left over from creation. They smell wrong deaths before they happen and try to snitch a bit of forgotten soul. Don't let them touch you. Because you're dead, they can sense you, but with that stone they will think you're a reaper and leave you alone."

My head bobbed up and down. Stay away from the black wings. Check.

"Cronus!" Barnabas begged, as Ron started downstairs again. "Please. Don't do this to me!"

"Find some wind and make the best of it," Ron muttered when he reached the downstairs landing and headed for the door. "It's only for a year."

He crossed the threshold into the sun. The light hit him, and he vanished, not all at once, but from the feet up as he moved into the light. The sun streaming into the house seemed to glitter, and then the distant mower roared to life.

I took a breath as the world began to turn again with the sound of birds, wind, and someone's radio. Bewildered, I stood beside Barnabas. "What does he mean, for a year?" I whispered. "Is that all I get?"

Barnabas looked me up and down, clearly peeved. "How should I know?"

From in my room came a startled "Madison? Is that you?"

"Dad!" I said, running into him as he came out. He turned it into a happy hug, his arms around me and smiling as he looked at Barnabas. "You must be the boy who brought Madison home last night. Seth, was it?"

Huh? I thought, shocked. He had already met Barnabas. And how had my dad gone from protective anger to congenial dad so fast? What about the accident? Or the hospital? The crashed car? *Me being dead?*

Barnabas shifted from foot to foot in what seemed like embarrassment, shooting my gaping-mouth expression a look to shut up. "No, sir. I'm Barnabas. One of Madison's friends. I was with her last night, too, after Josh left. It's good to meet you, sir. I just came over to see if Madison, uh, wanted to do anything today."

My dad looked proud that I had managed to make a friend without his help, but I was majorly confused. Clearing his throat as if trying to decide how to treat the first boyfriend of mine he'd had the chance to meet, he took Barnabas's extended hand. I stood and watched in wonder as they shook. Barnabas gave me a slight shrug, and I started to relax. It seemed everything had been wiped from my dad's thoughts and a fake memory of an uneventful evening put in its place—a teenager's dream of CYA to the max. Now all I had to do was figure out how Ron had done it. Just for future reference.

"Hey, do you have anything to eat around here?" Barnabas said, rubbing a hand across the back of his neck. "I feel like I haven't eaten in years."

Like magic, my dad fell into jovial-parent mode, talking about waffles as he stomped downstairs. Barnabas started after him, hesitating when I took his elbow and drew him to a stop.

"So the story is Seth brought me home and I watched TV the rest of the night?" I asked, wanting to know how much damage control I'd have to manage on my own. "I never went off that embankment?" I added when he nodded. "Who's going to remember last night? Anyone?"

"No one living," he said. "Ron takes time to be thorough. He must like you a lot." His gaze dropped to the stone about my neck. "Or maybe he simply likes your pretty new stone."

Feeling nervous all over again, I let go of his shirt and Barnabas schlumped after my dad—who was now yelling at us from the kitchen to find out if Barnabas could stay for breakfast. I straightened my dress, ran a hand over my mussed hair, and took slow, careful steps down after him. I felt really weird. A year. I had at least a year. I might not be alive, but by God I wasn't going to die all the way. I'd figure out how to use the stone I took and stay right where I was. Where I belonged. Here with my dad.

Watch me.

4

RESTLESS, I SAT ON the roof in the dark, flicking stones into the night as I tried to realign my thinking. I wasn't alive, but I wasn't altogether dead, either. As I'd suspected, a careful questioning of my dad spanning the entire day confirmed that not only did he not have a clue I had been dead at the hospital, but he didn't even remember the accident. He thought I'd ditched Josh when I found out I was a pity date, got a ride home with Seth and Barnabas, and watched TV all night, pouting in my costume.

He wasn't pleased I had ruined the rental, either. I didn't appreciate him taking the cost of it out of my allowance, but I wasn't going to complain. I was here, sort of alive, and that was all that mattered. My dad seemed surprised at my meek acceptance of my punishment, telling me I was growing up. Oh, if he only knew.

I watched my dad closely all day as I unpacked and put my stuff in drawers and on shelves. It was clear he knew something wasn't right, though he couldn't put his finger on it. He hardly let me out of his sight, coming upstairs to bring me snacks and pop until I could have screamed. More than once I caught him watching me with a frightened expression, hiding it when he saw me return his gaze. Dinner was a forced conversation over pork chops, and after picking at my food for a good twenty minutes, I excused myself, claiming I was tired after last night's prom.

Yeah. I ought to be tired, but I wasn't. No, it was two in the morning, and here I was out on the roof, pitching stones, pretending to be asleep as the world turned in a chilly darkness. Maybe I didn't need to sleep anymore.

Shoulders slumping, I picked another bit of tar off the shingles and flicked it at the chimney. It hit the metallic cap with a *ting*, ricocheting into the black. I scooted up the shallow pitch of the roof, then tugged my jeans back up where they ought to be.

A faint feeling of unease crept through me, starting from the tops of my hands in a soft prickling, slipping inward with an increasingly jagged spike. The sensation of being watched exploded into existence, and I spun, gasping, when Barnabas fell out of the tree arching overhead.

"Hey!" I shouted, heart thumping while he landed in a crouch like a cat. "How about some warning?"

He rose to stand in the moonlit darkness with his hands on his hips. There was a faint shimmer on him visible right along with his disgust. "If I had been a black reaper, you'd be dead."

"Yeah, well, I'm already dead, aren't I?" I said, flicking a stone at him. He didn't move as it arched over his shoulder. "What do you want?" I asked sullenly.

Instead of answering, he shrugged his narrow shoulders and looked east. "I want to know what you didn't tell Ron."

"Excuse me?"

He stood still as a rock, arms crossed over his chest and staring. "Seth said something to you in that car. It was the only time you were out of my sight. I want to know what it was. It might be the difference between you getting to play out this lie of being alive, or you getting carted off to a black court." Now he moved, his motion rough and angry. "I'm not going to fail again, and not because of you. You were important to Seth before you stole that stone. That's why he came to get you at the morgue. I want to know why."

I looked down at the stone, glittering in the moonlight, then shifted my gaze to my feet. The awkward angle of the roof made my ankles hurt. "He said my name had come up too many times in the affairs of men, and he was going to cull my soul."

Barnabas moved, coming to sit beside me with a lot of space between us. "He's done that. You're not a threat now that you're dead. Why did he come back for you?"

Reassured by his more relaxed posture, I looked at him, thinking his eyes seemed silver in the moonlight. "You won't tell?" I asked, wanting to trust him. I needed to talk to someone, and it wasn't like I could call up my old friends and vent about being dead—as entertaining as that might be.

Barnabas hesitated. "No, but I might try to persuade you to tell him yourself."

That I could deal with, and I took a slow breath. "He said that his ending my pathetic life was his ticket into a higher court. He came back to prove he had . . . culled me."

I waited for a reaction, but there was none. Finally I couldn't take it anymore and I lifted my head to meet his eyes. Barnabas was looking at me as if trying to figure out what it meant. Clearly not having an answer, he slowly said, "I think you should keep this to yourself for a while. He probably didn't mean anything by it. Forget it. Spend your time learning how to fit in."

"Yeah," I said with a sarcastic bark of laughter. "A new school is tons of fun."

"I meant fit in with the living."

"Oh." Okay. I was going to have to learn how to fit in,

not at a new school, but with the living. Swell. Remembering the disastrous dinner with my dad, I bit my lip. "Uh, Barnabas, am I supposed to eat?"

"Sure. If you want to. I don't. Not much, anyway," he said, sounding almost wistful. "But if you're like me, you'll never be hungry."

I tucked my short hair behind my ear. "How about sleep?"

At that, he smiled. "You can try. I can't manage it unless I am bored out of my mind."

I picked a bit of tar off the shingles and flicked it at the chimney again. "How come I don't have to eat?" I asked.

Barnabas turned to face me. "That stone of yours is giving off energy, and you're taking it in. Basking in it. Watch out for psychics. They'll think you're possessed."

"Mmmm," I murmured, wondering if I could get any useful information about what was really going on from a church, but they were wrong about grim reapers, so maybe they didn't know as much as they thought.

I sighed, sitting in the dark on my roof with a white reaper—my guardian angel. *Nice going, Madison*, I thought, wondering if my life—or death, rather—could get any more screwed up. I slowly fingered the stone that kept me somewhat alive, wondering what I was supposed to do now. Go to school. Do my homework. Be with my dad. Try to make sense of who I was and what

I was supposed to do. Nothing much had changed, really, apart from the no-eating-no-sleeping thing. So I had something worse than a black reaper gunning for me. I also had a guardian angel. And life, apparently, goes on, even if you aren't a participating part of it anymore.

Barnabas surprised me when he suddenly stood, and I leaned to look up at his height measured against the stars. "Let's go," he said, extending his hand. "I don't have anything to do tonight, and I'm bored. You're not a screamer, are you?"

My first thought was *screamer*? And then, *go where*? But what came out of my mouth was a lame, "I can't. I've been grounded. I can't set a foot outside the house apart from school until I pay for that costume." But I smiled, taking his hand and letting him help me rise. If Ron could make my dad forget I had died, I'd be willing to bet Barnabas could cover for me sneaking out a couple of hours.

"Yeah, well, I can't do anything about you being grounded," he said, "but where we're going, you won't be setting a foot anywhere."

"Huh?" I stammered, then stiffened when he moved behind me, taller because of the roof's pitch. "Hey!" I yelped when his arm went around me. But my protest vanished in shock at the gray shadow suddenly curving around us. It was real, smelling like my mom's feather pillow, and I gasped when his grip tightened and my feet left the roof in a downward drop of gravity.

"Holy crap!" I exclaimed as the world spread out beneath us, silver and black in the moonlight. "You have wings?"

Barnabas laughed, and with my stomach dropping in a tingling surge, we went higher.

Maybe . . . maybe this wasn't going to be so bad after all.

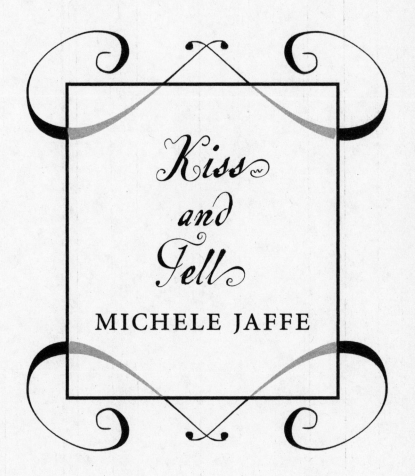

Kiss
and
Tell

MICHELE JAFFE

1

"SORRY THIS WASN'T MORE of a storybook ending," the man with his hands around her throat said, smiling, holding her eyes with his own as he choked her.

"If you're going to kill me, can't you just get on with it? This is kind of uncomfortable."

"What, my hands? Or the feeling that you're a failure—"

"I'm not a failure."

"—again."

She spit in his face.

"Still got some fire. I really admire that about you. I think you and I could have gotten along nicely. Unfortunately, there just isn't time."

She gave one last fight, clawing at his hands around her throat, his forearms, anything, but he didn't even flinch. Her fists fell hopelessly to her sides.

He leaned in so close to her face that she could feel him exhale. "Any last words?"

"Three: Listerine breath strips. You really need them."

He laughed and tightened the hands around her neck until they overlapped. "Good-bye."

For a second, his eyes burned into hers. Then she heard a sharp crack and felt herself fall to the floor as everything went black.

2

EIGHT HOURS EARLIER...

"*Foxy girls know that silence may be golden—but only for four seconds. Anything longer and you're heading for Awkward Avenue,*" Miranda read, then frowned at the book. "*If you feel the countdown creeping, make him an offer! A simple 'Would you like some nuts?' said with a smile can break the silence stagnation in a snap. Remember, foxy is as foxy does.*"

Miranda was starting to deeply distrust *How to Get—And Kiss!—Your Guy.*

Leaning against the side of the black Town Car parked in the loading zone at the Santa Barbara Municipal Airport that June evening, she thought of how totally thrilled she'd been when she'd found it at the bookstore. It looked like an and-they-all-lived-happily-ever-after dream come true in book form—who wouldn't want to learn "The Five Facial Expressions That Will Change Your Life" or "The Secrets of the Tongue Tantra Only Da Pros Know"?—but having done all the exercises, she wasn't convinced of the transformative powers of the Winsome Smile or spending half an hour a day sucking on a grape. It wasn't the first time a self-help book had let her down—*Procrastinate No More* and *Make Friends with YOU* had both been total disasters—but it was depressing because she'd had such high hopes this time. And because, as her best friend, Kenzi, recently pointed out, any senior in high school who acted like Miranda did around her crush really, really needed help.

She tried another passage. *"Rephrase one of his questions back to him, adding that hint of suggestion with a raised eyebrow. Or pick up the conversation with a pickup line! You:* Are we in the china section? *Him:* No, why? *You:* Because you are fine. *If china isn't your thing, this one never fails to launch—You:* Are you wearing space pants? *Him:* No, why? *You:* Because your butt is—"

"Hello, Miss Kiss."

Miranda looked up and found herself staring up at the cleft chin and tanned face of Deputy Sergeant Caleb Reynolds.

She must have been really distracted to not even have heard his heartbeat when he approached. It was distinctive, with a little echo at the end, kind of like a one-two-three cha-cha beat (she'd learned about the cha-cha beat from *You Can Dance!,* another massively unfortunate self-help experience). He'd probably have trouble with that when he got old, but at twenty-two it didn't seem to be stopping him from going to the gym, at least from the looks of his pecs, biceps, shoulders, forearms, wrists—

Stop staring.

Since she had an attack of Crazy Mouth whenever she tried to talk to a cute guy—let alone Santa Barbara's youngest sheriff's deputy, who was only four years older than she and who surfed every morning before work and who was cool enough to get away with wearing sunglasses even though it was almost 8:00 P.M.—she said, "Hi, deputy. Come here often?"

Causing him to frown. "No."

"No, you wouldn't, why would you? Me either. Well, not that often. Maybe once a week. Not often enough to know where the bathrooms are. Ha-ha!" Thinking, not for the first time, that life should come with a trapdoor. Just a little exit hatch you could disappear through when you'd utterly and completely mortified yourself. Or when you had spontaneous zit eruptions.

"Good book?" he asked, taking it from her and reading the subtitle, *"A Guide for Good Girls Who (Sometimes) Want to Be Bad,"* out loud.

But life did not come with a trapdoor.

"It's for a school project. Homework. On, um, mating rituals."

"Thought crime was more your thing." He hit her with one of his half smiles, too cool to pull out a big grin. "You planning on foiling any more convenience store heists any time soon?"

That had been a mistake. Not stopping the guys who'd held up Ron's 24-Hour Open Market #3, but sticking around long enough to let the police see her. For some reason they'd found it hard to believe that she'd just been leaning against the lamppost when it fell across the front of the robbers' car as it sped through the intersection. It was sad how suspicious people were, especially people in law enforcement. And school administration. But she'd learned a lot since then.

"I'm trying to keep it to one heist a month," she said, hoping for a light, ha-ha-I'm-just-kidding-*foxy-is-as-foxy-does* tone. "Today it's just my regular job, VIP airport pickup." Miranda heard his cha-cha heartbeat speed up slightly. Maybe he thought VIPs were cool.

"That boarding school you go to, Chatsworth Academy? They let you off campus any time you want or only certain days?"

"Wednesday and Saturday afternoons, if you're a senior. We don't have classes then," she said and heard his heartbeat pick up more.

"Wednesday and Saturday afternoons free. What do you do for fun?"

Was he asking her out? No. Way. NOWAYNOWAY-

NOWAY! *Flirt!* she ordered herself. Winsome Smile! Say something! Anything! Be foxy! Now!

"What do *you* do for fun?" she repeated his question back to him, raising one eyebrow for that hint of suggestion.

He seemed taken aback for a second, then said very formally, "I work, Miss Kiss."

Please give a warm welcome to Miranda Kiss, our new Miss Idiot Girl of the year, she thought. Said: "Of course. Me too. I mean, I'm either driving clients or at team practice. I'm one of Tony Bosun's Bee Girls? The Roller Derby team? That's why I do this," meaning to point to the Town Car but bashing it with her hand instead. "You have to be a driver for Tony's company, 5Bs Luxury Transport, to be on the team. We usually only have games on the weekends, but we practice on Wednesdays, sometimes on other days . . . ," Crazy Mouth trailed off.

"I've seen the Bees play. That's a professional team, isn't it? They let a high school student play?"

Miranda swallowed. "Oh, sure. Of course."

He looked at her over the top of his sunglasses.

"Okay, I had to lie to get on the team. Tony thinks I'm twenty. You won't tell him, will you?"

"He believed you were twenty?"

"He needed a new jammer."

Deputy Reynolds chuckled. "So you're the jammer? You're good. I can see why he might have made an exception." Eyeing her some more. "I never would have recognized you."

"Well, you know, we wear those wigs and the gold masks over our eyes so we all look the same." It was one of the things she liked about Roller Derby, the anonymity, the fact that no one knew who you were, what your skills were. It made her feel invulnerable, safe. No one could single you out for . . . anything.

Deputy Reynolds took his sunglasses all the way off now to look at her. "So you put on one of those red, white, and blue satin outfits? The ones with the short skirts and that cute cape? I'd like to see that sometime."

He smiled at her, right into her eyes, and her knees went weak and her mind started playing out a scenario involving him without his shirt but with a pitcher of maple syrup and a big—

"Well, there's my lady," he said. "Catch you." And then walked away.

—stack of pancakes. Miranda watched him go up to a woman in her early twenties—thick blond hair, thin but muscular—put his arm around her, and kiss her neck. The kind of woman whose bras had tags that said, SIZE 36C, not MADE BY SANRIO in them. Heard him saying excitedly, "Wait until we get to the house. I've got some amazing new toys, something special just for you," his voice husky, heart racing.

As he passed Miranda, he lifted his chin in her direction and said, "You stay out of trouble."

"Yeah, you too," Crazy Mouth told him. Miranda wanted to bang her head against the top of the car at how *idiotic* she was. She tried to give a Lite Laff (expression number four from the book) but ended up making herself choke instead.

When they were across the parking lot, she heard the woman asking who she was and heard Deputy Reynolds say, "The local Town Car driver."

"She's the driver?" the woman said. "Looks like one of those girls from Hawaiian Airlines you used to date, but younger. And cuter. You know how your judgment gets around cute young girls. You're sure I don't need to be concerned?"

Miranda heard him laugh, the genuine amusement in his voice as he said, "Her? Baby, she's just a high school student who has a crush on me. Trust me, you've got nothing to worry about."

And thought: Trap. Door. Now. Please.

Sometimes having superhearing supersucked.

3

MIRANDA LOVED THE SANTA Barbara airport, the way it looked more like an Acapulco Joe's Cantina than an official building with its adobe-style walls, cool terra-cotta floor, loopy blue and gold tile, and bougainvillea careening down the walls. It was small, so planes just parked where they landed and had staircases wheeled out to them, with only a chain-link fence separating people waiting for someone from the people coming off the plane.

Pulling the welcome sign out of the Town Car, she checked the name on it—CUMEAN—and held it up in the direction of the disembarking passengers. As she waited, she listened to a woman in the gold Lexus SUV four cars behind her talking on her phone, saying, "If she gets off the plane, I'll know. He'd better have his checkbook ready," then tilted her head to focus on the low *srloop srloop srloop* sound of a snail slithering across the still-warm pavement toward a bunch of ivy.

She still remembered the exact moment she realized that not everyone heard the things she heard, that she wasn't normal. She'd already spent the first half of her seventh-grade year at Saint Bartolomeo School—the part after the screening of the *Your Body Is Changing: Womanhood* video—puzzled by all the changes they didn't list, like uncontrolled bursts of speed and randomly crushing objects you were just trying to pick up and hitting your head on the ceiling of the gym when you were doing jumping jacks and suddenly being able to see dust particles on people's clothes. But since Sister Anna answered all her questions with "Stop joking, child," Miranda thought they must just be so obvious the movie didn't need to mention them. It was only when she'd tried to earn Johnnie Voight's undying affection by warning him not to cheat off of Cynthia Riley again because, based on the sound of her pencil five seats away, she always got the wrong answers, that Miranda learned just how "differently abled" she was. Instead of falling on his knees and declaring that she was his goddess in a training bra and plaid skirt, Johnnie had called her a freak, then a nosy bitch, and tried to beat her up.

That was how she'd first learned how dangerous powers were, the way they could make you an outcast.

And also that she was stronger than boys her age, and that they didn't think that was cool or even good. And neither did school administrators.

Since then she'd become expert at acting normal, being careful. Had mastered her powers. Or she'd thought she had, until seven months earlier when—

Miranda pushed the memory aside and turned her attention back to the people at the airport. To her job. She watched a little girl with blond ringlets sitting on her dad's shoulders standing next to the path and waving as a woman walked from the plane toward them, now shouting, "Mommy, Mommy, I missed you!"

She watched the happy family hug and felt like someone had socked her in the stomach. One of the advantages of going to boarding school, Miranda thought, was that you didn't get invited over to people's houses, never had to see them acting like normal families, having breakfast together. For some reason, whenever she imagined truly happy families, they were always eating breakfast.

Plus people who had normal families didn't go to Chatsworth Academy, "The Premier Boarding Experience in Southern California." Or, as Miranda liked to think of it, Child Warehouse, the place where parents (or in her case, guardians) stored their children until they needed them for something.

With the possible exception of her roommate, Kenzi.

She and Kenzi Chin had lived together for four years, since their freshman year, longer than Miranda had lived with almost anyone. Kenzi came from a perfect-eat-breakfast-together family, had perfect skin, perfect grades, perfect everything, and Miranda would have been forced to hate her if Kenzi wasn't also so completely loyal and kind. And a tinsy bit insane.

Like earlier that afternoon when Miranda walked into their room and found her standing on her head, wearing only underpants, with her entire body slathered in drying mint-colored mud.

"I am so going to be in therapy for the rest of my life to get this image out of my mind," Miranda told her.

"You're going to need to be in therapy that long anyway to deal with your messed-up family. I'm just giving you some TTD material to talk about." Kenzi knew more about Miranda's family history than anyone else at Chatsworth, almost all of it fabricated. The part about it being messed up, though, was true.

Kenzi also really liked acronyms and invented new ones all the time. As she dropped her bag and collapsed on her bed, Miranda asked, "TTD?"

"Totally Top Drawer." Then Kenzi said, "I can't believe you're not coming to prom. I always pictured us going together."

"I don't think Beth would like that too much. You know, being the third wheel."

Beth was Kenzi's girlfriend. "Don't even talk to me about that creature," she said now, giving a fake shudder. "The Beth and Kenzi Show is officially canceled."

"As of when?"

"What time is it?"

"Three thirty-five."

"Two hours and six minutes ago."

"Oh, so it'll be back on by prom."

"Of course."

Kenzi's "cancellations" happened about once a week and never lasted more than four hours. She thought the drama of breakups and the thrill of reconciliation kept a relationship fresh. And in some weird way it seemed to work, because she and Beth were the happiest couple Miranda knew. More perfection.

"Anyway, stop trying to change the subject. I think you're making a grave mistake by missing prom."

"Yeah, I'm sure I'll never forgive myself."

"I'm serious."

"Why? What's the big deal? It's a big dance with a dorky theme. You know I'm dancelexic and should not be allowed out on a dance floor near other people."

"A Sweet Salute to the Red, White, and Blue isn't dorky, it's patriotic. And you do okay with the Hustle."

"I think Libby Geer would disagree with you. If her mouth weren't still wired shut."

"Whatever, prom isn't just a big dance. It's a rite of

passage, a moment when we move from who we were into the vastness of the adults we're going to become, throwing off the weight of our youthful insecurities to—"

"—get drunk and maybe lucky. Depending on your definition of luck."

"You'll be sorry if you don't come. Do you really want to grow up miserable and filled with regret?"

"Yes, please! Besides, I have to work."

"TGI as If. You're hiding behind your job again. You could so get one Saturday off. At least be honest about why you're not going."

Miranda gave Kenzi Innocent Eyes, expression number two from the kissing book. "I don't know what you mean."

"Don't look at me like you're My Little Pony. I have four letters for you: W-I-L-L."

"And I have four letters for you: N-O-P-E. Oh and four more: M-Y-O—"

But Kenzi just went on, ignoring her, something she did professionally. "It's true that Will might need to be vaccinated or screened for diseases after going with Ariel, but I can't believe you're giving up that easily."

Will Javelin filled up about 98 percent of Miranda's dreams. She'd been trying to cut it out since she learned he was going to the prom with Ariel—"I named my new breasts after my family's country houses, does your family have any country houses, Miranda? Oh right, I forgot, you're a *foster child*"—West, of the West-Sugar-Is-Best! fortune, but it was a challenge. To avoid bad karma Miranda said, "There's nothing wrong with Ariel."

"Yeah, nothing that couldn't be cured with an exorcism." Kenzi came out of her headstand, planting her feet on the floor. She reached for her towel. "At least promise you'll come to the after-party. At Sean's parents' place on the beach? You will, right? We're all going to hang around and watch the sun rise. It will give you a chance to talk to Will outside of school. And when are you going to tell me what happened between you two that other night, anyway? Why are you being so MLAS about it?"

Miranda knew that one. "I'm not being My Lips Are Sealed," she said, picking up a pile of papers on the bookshelf between her and Kenzi's beds and straightening them.

"You're doing that thing again. The thing where you pretend to be Holly Homemaker to avoid having a discussion."

"Maybe." Miranda was looking at the papers now, photocopies of newspaper articles from the past half year. "*Purse snatcher caught by mysterious Good Samaritan, found bound to fence with yo-yo*," the first and most recent said. Then, from a few months before, "*Get a grip: Stickup foiled when robber loses control of gun. Witness says Pez dispenser 'came out of nowhere' to knock weapon from assailant's hand."* Finally, from seven months earlier, *"Convenience store heist getaway halted by falling lightpost; two arrested."* She started to get a sinking feeling in her stomach.

At least it was only three out of, what, a dozen different incidents she told herself. But that didn't really make her feel better. No one was supposed to link *any* of those events together. Ever.

The convenience store was the first one. It was dusk, fog coming off the ocean, the streetlights making misty halos in the air. She'd been driving down a side street in Santa Barbara on her way to roller derby practice when she'd heard the threats from inside Ron's 24-Hour Open Market #3 and just . . . acted. She'd had no control over what she did, it was like she was in a dream, her body knowing exactly what to do, where the robbers would go, how to stop them. Coming back to her the way the words from a favorite song did even if you hadn't heard it in years. Only she had no idea where it was coming back *from.*

She'd spent the three days following the convenience store incident in bed, curled in a ball, trembling. She told Kenzi she had the flu, but really what she had was terror. She was terrified of the powers she suddenly couldn't restrain.

Terrified because using them felt so good. So right. Like she was alive for the first time.

Terrified because she knew what could happen if people found out. To her. And to—

She waved the copies toward Kenzi, demanding, "What are you doing with these?"

"Whoa, Drill Sergeant Kiss in the house," Kenzi said, saluting. "All due respect, ma'am, but as they say in the military, SSTB. You won't get away with changing the subject just by using your scary voice."

SSTB stood for So Sad Too Bad. Miranda couldn't not laugh. "If I were trying to change the subject, army of one, I'd point out that the stuff on your body is flaking all over the rug your mother's decorator tracked over three continents because it supposedly belonged to Lucy Lawless. I seriously want to know, why are you interested in street crime in Santa Barbara?"

Kenzi stepped from the rug onto the wood floor. "Not street crime in Santa Barbara, *foiled* street crime. It's for my journalism final project. Some people are saying there's a mystical force at work. Maybe even Santa Barbara come back herself."

"Can't it just be a coincidence? Criminals mess up all the time, right?"

"People don't like coincidences. Like the way it's no coincidence that you are trying to make me talk about this rather than answer my questions about what happened with you and Will. One minute it looks like you two are totally—and I might add, finally—hooking up and the next you are back here in our room. Ruining, I might also add, a totally ace romantic evening for me."

"I *did* tell you," Miranda groaned. "It was nothing. Nothing happened."

Slouching against the Town Car now as the last of the daylight faded, Miranda thought that *nothing* was an understatement. It had been worse than nothing. That expression on Will's face, the one that hovered between you've-got-something-green-caught-in-your-teeth and oh-hello-Professor-Crazy, a mixture of horror and, well, horror, when she'd finally gotten up the guts to—

That's when it hit her. The articles on Kenzi's desk had all come out on Thursdays, reporting on things that had happened—things she'd done—on Wednesdays.

"Wednesday and Saturday afternoons free," she heard Caleb saying, repeating her words.

That was bad. That was really bad. She was going to have to lay low.

The gold Lexus SUV behind her pulled away from the curb and Miranda could hear the couple inside fighting over the sound of their air conditioner. The woman at the wheel turning her head to yell at her husband—*Don't lie to me! I know you were with her!*—hitting the gas hard right as the family with the little blond girl stepped into the crosswalk in front of her . . .

Afterward no one was really sure what had happened.

One second the car was careening toward the family in the crosswalk, the next there was a blur and they were on the curb, bewildered but safe.

As she watched the gold SUV speed off into the distance, Miranda felt the adrenaline thrill she always got after she'd acted without thinking, saved someone. It was addictive, like a drug.

And dangerous, like a drug, she reminded herself.

I think you should get yourself a dictionary. That is not what "laying low" means.

Shut up. It was only a handspring and a little push. Hardly some big tactical maneuver.

You shouldn't have done it. It was too risky. You're not invisible, you know.

But I wasn't seen. It was fine.

This time.

Miranda wondered if everyone had a voice in their head permanently set to the U-Suck channel.

What are you trying to do, anyway? Do you think you can save everyone? When you couldn't even—

Shut *up.*

"What?" a girl's voice asked and Miranda was startled to realize she'd spoken aloud, and someone was standing there.

The girl was about Miranda's height but younger, maybe fourteen, and dressed like she'd been studying early Madonna videos and wanted to be sure that if mesh shirts worn over bras, fingerless gloves, teased hair, thick black eyeliner, rubber bracelets, petticoat skirts with fishnets, and ankle boots came back in style, she'd be ready.

"I'm sorry," Miranda said, "I was talking to myself." Not exactly how the Mature Driver Person she was supposed to be should act.

"Oh." The girl held the sign with the word CUMEAN on it out to Miranda. "You'll want this. And this," she said, handing her a small square box.

Miranda took the sign but shook her head at the box. "That's not mine."

"It must be. And me, too. I mean, I'm Sibby Cumean." She pointed at the sign.

Miranda pocketed the box to open the back door for the girl, wondering what kind of parent let their fourteen-year-old get picked up by a stranger at eight at night.

"Can't I ride in front?"

"Clients prefer the back," Miranda said in her most professional voice.

"What you really mean is that you prefer it when they ride in the back. But what if I want to ride in the front? Don't clients get to do what they want?"

5Bs Luxury Transport was named after a set of principles the owner, Tony Bosun, had made up—B on time, B polite, B accommodating, B discreet, B sure to get paid. Even though Miranda suspected he'd come up with them when he was drunk late one night, she tried to follow the rules and she was pretty sure this counted as B accommodating. She moved to open the front door.

The girl shook her head. "Never mind. I'll stay in back."

Miranda plastered on a smile. What a rad day she was having! Her VIP client was a tiny demon, her dream guy was going to the prom with someone else, and the sheriff's deputy she had a crush on not only knew it but joked about it with his girlfriend! Awesome.

At least, she told herself, things couldn't possibly get any worse.

Oh, now you've done it.

Shut up.

4

SIBBY CUMEAN STARTED TALKING as soon as they got out of the airport.

"How long have you been driving people around?" she asked Miranda.

"A year."

"Did you grow up here?"

"No."

"Do you have any brothers?"

"No."

"Any sisters?"

"N—no."

"Do you like driving?"

"Yes."

"Do you have to wear that boring black suit?"

"Yes."

"How old are you?"

"Twenty."

"Um, not."

"Fine. Eighteen."

"Have you ever had sex?"

Miranda cleared her throat. "I don't think that question is appropriate." She heard herself sound like Dr. Trope, the assistant head of school, with the voice he used to tell her he wasn't listening to another excuse about why she was late getting back to campus, rules were made for a reason and that reason wasn't so she could flout them for her amusement; and speaking of late, did she plan at some point to decide what she was going to do next year or just irresponsibly forfeit her place at the several top-tier colleges she'd been accepted to, making the school look bad and herself look worse; and really he didn't know what had gotten into her recently, where was the Miranda Kiss who was going to be a doctor and save the world, who was a credit to the school and herself, rather than the one who was on her way to being expelled—is that what you really want, young lady? A voice she knew well since she seemed to have been hearing it at least once a week since early November.

"You're a virgin," Sibby announced, like she was confirming a sad fact she'd long suspected.

"That's not—"

"Do you at least have a boyfriend?"

"Not at this—"

"A girlfriend?"

"No."

"Do you have any friends? You're not really very good at conversation."

Miranda was beginning to understand why the girl's relatives hadn't come to the airport for her.

"I have lots of friends."

"Sure. I believe you. What do you do for fun?"

"Answer questions."

"Please never try to be funny again." Sibby leaned forward. "Have you ever thought of wearing some black eyeliner? It would be an improvement."

B polite! "Thanks."

"Can you pull up?"

"Um, we're at a stoplight."

"Just go forward a tiny—perfect."

Looking in the side mirror, Miranda saw that Sibby had rolled down her window and was leaning out, saying now to the guys in the jeep next to them, "Where are you boys going?"

The guys answered, "A little moonlight surfing. Want to come, goddess?"

"I'm not a goddess. Do you think I look like one?"

"I can't tell. Maybe if you take off your shirt."

"Maybe if you give me a kiss."

Miranda hit the button to roll up the window.

"What are you doing?" Sibby demanded. "You could have broken my hand."

"Put your seat belt on, please."

"Put your seat belt on, please," Sibby mimicked, slumping back into the seat. "Oh my gods, I was just trying to be sociable."

"Until we get to your destination, no more socializing."

"Have you listened to yourself recently? You sound like you're eighty, not eighteen." She scowled at Miranda in the mirror. "I thought you were a driver, not a jailer."

"It's my job to make sure you get where you're going in a safe and timely manner. That's printed on the card you'll find in your seat pocket, by the way."

"How is kissing some boys going to make me unsafe?"

"A million different ways. What if they have an invisible mouth fungus? Or DeathLip."

"There's no such thing as DeathLip."

"Are you sure?"

"You're just jealous because I know how to have fun and you don't. *Virgin*."

Miranda rolled her eyes but kept quiet, listening to cell phone conversations from the cars behind them, a woman telling someone that the gardener was on his way, a guy saying in a mystical voice, "I see a mysterious stranger coming for you, I can't quite tell if it's a man or a woman." Another man talking to someone about how he wanted to take that bitch out of the will and it didn't matter if she was his mother's favorite dog—

She was interrupted suddenly by Sibby shouting, "In-n-Out Burger! We have to stop."

B accommodating!

Miranda agreed to let Sibby order her own at the drive-through, then regretted it when she heard the girl saying to the guy taking the order, "Do I get a discount if I let you kiss me?"

"Okay, seriously, were you raised on Crazycake? Why do you want to kiss all these guys you don't even know?" Miranda asked.

"There aren't that many boys where I come from. And what does knowing them have to do with it? Kissing is great. I kissed four boys on the airplane. I'm hoping to make it twenty-five before the end of the day."

She added the two working the drive-through lane when she got her burger.

"Are all hamburgers that delicious?" she asked when they were on the road again.

Miranda glanced at her in the rearview mirror. "You've never had a burger before? Where do you live?"

"The mountains," Sibby answered quickly, and Miranda picked up a slight rise in her heart rate, suggesting that she was lying and not used to it. Which seemed hugely unlikely—the not-used-to-it part—for someone who had a case of acute Boy Crazy like this girl. Her parents couldn't possibly let her run around—

Oh So Very Much Not Your Problem, Miranda reminded herself. B discreet.

Sibby tried to solicit kisses from four other guys as they drove. They were a mile from the drop-off point and Miranda was thinking that the ride could not be over soon enough when Sibby shrieked, "Oh my gods, a doughnut store! I've always wanted to try doughnuts, too. Can we stop? Pleasepleasepleasepleaseplease?"

They were already almost an hour late but Miranda couldn't deny anyone a doughnut. Even someone who said, "Oh my god*s*." But pulling in, she saw a group of guys sitting at a table inside and decided that it would be dangerous to let Sibby near them if she wanted to get out of there in under forty minutes. "I'll go in and get them, you stay here."

Sibby had seen the guys, too. "No way, I'm coming in."

"Either your butt stays in the car, Kissing Bandit, or the doughnuts stay in the store."

"I don't think that's a nice way to talk to customers."

"Feel free to use my phone to file a complaint while I'm inside. Do we have a deal?"

"Fine. But will you at least roll down the window?" Miranda hesitated. Sibby said, "Look, Grandma, I promise I'll keep my butt in the car, I just don't want to suffocate. Gods."

When Miranda came out, Sibby had wedged herself in the window with her body and legs outside the car and her rear hanging back into it, and was deeply involved in kissing a blond guy.

"Excuse me," Miranda said, tapping the guy on the shoulder.

He turned around kind of hazy, looked her up and down. "Hello, dream girl. You want a kiss, too? I could do something really special with lips like yours. You wouldn't even have to pay me a dollar."

"Thanks, but no." Looking at Sibby now. "I thought we'd agreed that—"

"—my butt would stay in the car. Where, if you bothered to look, you would see it is."

Miranda turned away so Sibby wouldn't see her crack up.

She handed Sibby the doughnuts and slid into the driver's seat. Once Sibby had wiggled back through the window, Miranda caught her eye in the rearview. "You were paying guys to kiss you?"

"So what?" Sibby glared. "Not all of us can get kissed for free." More glaring, then, "You barely have boobs. My boobs are bigger than yours. It makes no sense."

Sibby got quiet, not even eating her doughnut. From time to time she'd sigh dramatically.

Miranda started feeling a little sorry. Maybe she had been acting like a grandma. She looked at *How to Get—And Kiss—Your Guy* on the seat next to her. *Maybe you're jealous she's four years younger than you but has already kissed more guys in one day than you'll probably date in your whole life even if you get a boob job and live to be two trillion.*

Shut up, U-Suck channel.

She should be nice, make conversation. "How many kisses is it total now?"

Sibby kept her eyes on her lap. "Ten." Looking up to add, "But I only paid six of them. And one of them I only gave a quarter."

"Nice work."

Miranda saw Sibby look up suspiciously, like she thought she was being made fun of, decide she wasn't, and start picking at her doughnut. After a while she said, "Can I ask you a question?"

"You're asking permission now?"

"For real, just please stop trying to be funny. It's painful."

"Thanks for the hot tip. Did you have a question or—"

"Why didn't you want to kiss that boy back there? The one who wanted to kiss you?"

"I guess he's not my type."

"What's your type?"

Miranda thought of Deputy Reynolds—blue eyes and cleft jaw and shaggy blond hair, getting up every morning to go surfing. The kind of guy who always wore sunglasses or looked at you with his eyes half closed and was too cool for smiling. Then pictured Will with his dark, maple-syrup-color skin, short curly hair, huge boyish smile, and abs that rippled when he stood talking, shirtless, with the other players after lacrosse practice, body glimmering in the sun, his laugh ringing out and making her feel like she felt when she saw butter melting on perfectly cooked Belgian waffles.

Not that she routinely jumped up onto the roof of the marine biology lab when no one was looking to watch this. (Weekly.)

"I don't know, it's more a feeling than a type," Miranda said finally.

"How many boys have you kissed? A hundred?"

"Uh, no."

"Two hundred?"

Miranda felt herself blushing and hoped Sibby couldn't see. "Keep guessing."

They pulled up to the address she'd been given, an hour and fifteen minutes later than they should have, the first time she'd ever dropped a client off late.

When Miranda opened the car door for her, Sibby asked, "Is kissing a boy who's your type really different than kissing just any boy?"

"It's complicated." Miranda was surprised at how relieved she was that she wouldn't have to go into it more, admit to this girl that, actually, she had no idea.

The place looked more like a government safe house for witnesses than a home, she thought, walking Sibby to the door. It was like the dictionary definition of *nondescript*, sandwiched between a house with Snow White and the Seven Dwarves enacting the Nativity on the front lawn on one side, and one with a pink-and-orange swing set on the other. The only thing you noticed about this house was that there were thick curtains hanging in the front windows so you couldn't see in, and a six-foot-tall solid wood fence blocking off the backyard so you couldn't get in. The street was filled with noises—Miranda heard BBQs sizzling, conversations, someone watching *Beauty and the Beast* in Spanish—but this house was silent, as though it had been soundproofed.

She registered a low humming coming from the side, like an air conditioner but not quite. Glancing up, she saw that none of the power lines connected to this house. None of the phone lines, either. A generator. Whoever lived here was living off the grid. All in all, the whole place was really cozy, if cozy meant creepy and cultish.

And the woman who opened the front door? Exactly what you'd expect of someone creepy and cultish, Miranda thought. She had graying hair pulled back in a loose bun and was wearing a long skirt and kind of shapeless sweater. She could have been anywhere from thirty to sixty years old, it was impossible to tell because she was wearing a pair of huge bifocals with unflattering square frames that magnified her eyes and covered half her face. She looked completely harmless, like a school-teacher who'd dedicated her life to caring for an aging relative and whose one indulgence was a secret crush on Mr. Rochester from *Jane Eyre*.

Or almost like that. Like that was the look she'd been going for. But there was something wrong, some tiny thing that did not quite match, one tiny detail that wasn't right.

So. Not. Your. Business.

Miranda said good-bye, took her $1.00 tip—"Because you were really quite late, dear"—and drove away.

She was half a block away when she slammed on the brakes and sprinted back to the house.

5

W HAT DO YOU THINK *you're doing?* she asked herself. Rhetorically, since she was already up the Snow-White-and-the-Seven-Dwarves-Do-Baby-Jesus neighbor's tree and staring into the yard of the house where she'd left Sibby.

I can't wait to hear you say to the cops, "Yes, officer, I know I was trespassing but that woman was very suspicious because she was wearing false eyelashes."

With a full Creepy Cult costume. They just didn't go. Plus she had a hole for a nose piercing. And a French manicure.

Maybe she just has really big pores! And a love of dated manicures!

She wasn't what she was posing as.

Is this about helping someone or having an excuse not

to show up at prom and see Will with his face nuzzled in Ariel's huge, soft—

Shut up, U-Suck.

I was going to say hair.

You are so not funny.

You are so not brave.

There were two guys sitting in the backyard, leaning across a picnic table toward each other with a book between them, both in T-shirts and khakis and Teva sandals, one of them wearing thick black-framed glasses, the other one with a scraggly beard. They looked like two geeky college guys playing Dungeons and Dragons and sounded like it too when the one wearing glasses said, "That's not how it works. It says in the Book of Rules she can't see for herself, only for other people. You know, like genies with wishes, how they can't grant their own." Except they each had a large automatic rifle lying on the table next to them and Miranda could see shooting targets set up on the fence.

So what? There are armed geeks. Maybe they're Sibby's protection. Go home. Sibby doesn't need you. She's fine.

If she's fine, why isn't she out there trying to kiss the two boys?

Miranda strained to hear something from inside the house but it was definitely soundproofed. A couple came out of sliding doors onto the patio away from the Geek Guys, a woman smoking a cigarette in short, tense puffs and a man. Miranda almost fell out of the tree when she recognized the woman as the cult lady, only now without the glasses, skirt, or sweater and with her hair down.

Which doesn't mean anything.

The woman whispered, "We still need the girl to tell us the location, Byron."

"She will."

"She hasn't yet."

"I told you, even if I can't get her to talk, the Gardener can. He's good at that."

The woman again: "I don't like that he brought a partner. That wasn't part of the plan. Does she get a cut—"

The man called Byron cut her off. "Put that out and be quiet, we have company." He pointed to the Geek Guys scrambling over to join them.

The woman crushed her cigarette out under her foot and kicked it away.

"Is She all right?" Bearded Geek asked breathlessly, pronouncing *She* like it should be capitalized.

"Yes," the man assured him. "She's resting after her ordeal."

Oh, they could *not* be talking about Sibby. Ordeal? No way.

"Has She said anything?" Glasses Geek asked.

The man said, "Just expressed how very grateful She is to be here."

Miranda almost snorted.

Bearded Geek said, "Will we be able to see Her?"

"When the Transition happens."

The geeks wandered off in a blissful daze and Miranda decided this was the weirdest thing she'd ever seen.

But it proved that Sibby was in no danger. These people clearly worshipped Her. Which meant it was time—

"Why is he called the Gardener, anyway?" Fake Eyelash woman asked the man.

"I believe because he's good at pulling things out."

"Things?"

"Teeth, nails. Joints. That's how he gets people to talk."

—time to find Sibby.

Miranda dropped out of the tree into the neighbor's yard and found herself looking down the barrel of an automatic rifle.

6

"PUT THEM UP," Glasses Geek said. "I mean your arms."

Miranda did what he said because his hands were shaking so much she was afraid he'd shoot her by accident.

"Who are you? What are you doing here?" he demanded in a voice that shook almost as much as his hands.

"I just wanted to get a glimpse of Her," she said, hoping she made it sound right.

He narrowed his eyes. "How did you know She was here?"

"The Gardener told me, but I didn't know where She was being kept so I climbed up that tree to look."

"Which affiliate are you with?"

I knew this would end in tears. What now, smarty pants?

Miranda raised an eyebrow and said, "Which affiliate are *you* with?" Adding for good measure, "I mean, I would remember a guy like you if I'd seen you before."

It worked! She saw him swallow hard, his Adam's apple bobbing up and down. She would never doubt *How to Get—And Kiss—Your Guy* again! He said, "I'd remember you, too."

She hit him with a dose of Winsome Smile and saw the Adam's apple do some more moving. She said, "If I give you my hand to shake, will you shoot me?"

He chortled and put down the gun. "No," still chortling. Holding out his hand now. "I'm Craig."

"Hi, Craig, I'm Miranda," she said, taking it. Then flipped him onto his back and knocked him out cold in a single silent move.

She looked at her hand for a second in shock. She'd *definitely* never done that before. That had been very cool.

If you're going to be an idiot and risk everything, you might as well do what you came for. You know, instead of just staring at the guy you knocked out?

She bent to whisper, "Sorry. Take three aspirin for your head when you wake up and you'll feel better," in his ear, and moved around the edge of the safe house.

There must have been an open window because she

could hear voices here, the man who had been outside before now saying to someone, "Are you comfortable?"

And Sibby answering, "No. I don't like this couch. I can't believe this is the nicest room in the house. It looks like a place for a grandma."

Heh!

Miranda followed the sound of Sibby's voice and found herself standing in front of one of the street-facing plate-glass windows, looking through a gap in dark blue drapes into a living room. There was a spindly-looking couch, chair, and coffee table. Sibby was in the chair, her profile to Miranda, with a plate of Oreos in front of her. She looked fine.

The man was perched on the couch, smiling at Sibby, saying, "So, where are we supposed to drop you?"

Sibby took the top cookie off the Oreo and ate it. "I'll tell you later."

The man kept smiling. "I'd like to know so I can plan the route. We can't be too careful."

"Oh my gods, there's like hours before we go. I want to watch some TV."

Miranda heard the man's heart speed up and saw his hand flex but he kept his tone light when he said, "Of course." Then added, "As soon as you tell me where we're taking you."

Sibby frowned at him. "Are you deaf or something? I said I'd tell you later."

"It's in your best interest to talk to me. Otherwise I'm afraid I'll have to bring in someone else. Someone a bit more . . . forceful."

"Fine. But while I'm waiting, can I please watch TV? Tell me you get cable. Oh gods, if you don't have MTV, I'm going to be really pissed."

The man stood up with an expression on his face like he wanted to break something, then abruptly turned to face the door. Miranda heard footsteps coming toward the room from the hallway, and with them a familiar cha-cha heartbeat. Two seconds later Deputy Sergeant Caleb Reynolds burst through the door.

See? Sibby's in no danger. The police are here. Scram.

Deputy Reynolds said to the man, "What's taking so long?"

"She won't talk."

"I'm sure she'll change her mind." His heartbeat picked up.

Sibby glanced at him. "Who are you?"

Caleb said, "I'm the Gardener."

This was extremely not good, Miranda decided.

"I wasn't very impressed with the front lawn," Sibby told him.

"I'm not that kind of Gardener. It's a nickname. They call me that because—"

"Actually, I'm not even vaguely interested. I don't know what you're planning, Plant Boy—"

"Gardener," he corrected, going a touch red.

"—but if you need to know where I'm supposed to be picked up by the Overseer, then you have to keep me alive, right? So you can't exactly threaten me with death."

"Not death, no. But pain." He addressed the man. "Go get me my tools, Byron."

As the man left the room, Sibby said, "I'm not going to tell you anything."

Deputy Reynolds circled around so he was leaning over her chair, his back to the window.

"Listen to me—" he said, his heartbeat slowing down suddenly.

Miranda did a round-off, smashing through the window feet first, then knocked him unconscious with a side kick to the neck before he could turn around. She bent to whisper, "Sorry," in his ear, decided as punishment not to tell him about the aspirins, grabbed Sibby, sprinted to the car, and stepped on the gas.

7

"HE DIDN'T EVEN KNOW you were there," Sibby said. "He never even knew who hit him."

"That was the idea." They were parked next to an abandoned Amtrak maintenance building on an old part of the train tracks that was completely hidden from the street. It was the place Miranda had started coming seven months earlier to work out all her new crazy energy and try things she couldn't practice anywhere else—Roller Derby was great for speed, balance, gymnastics, and shoving moves, but you weren't supposed to use advanced judo. Or weapons.

She could make out marks from her last crossbow exercise on the side of the building, and the piece of railroad track she'd tied in a knot the day after Will rejected her was still lying on the ground. She'd never seen anyone else here, and she was sure she and Sibby would be pretty much invisible as long as they stayed parked.

"Where did you learn to knock people out like that?" Sibby asked, sprawled out over the backseat. "Can you teach me?"

"No."

"Why not? Just one move?"

"Absolutely not."

"Why did you say you were sorry after you hit him?"

Miranda swiveled to face her. "It's my turn to ask questions. Who wants to kill you and why?"

"Gods, I don't know. It could be a ton of people. It's not like that, how you think it is."

"What's it like then?"

"It's complicated. But if we can just hang out until four in the morning, there's a place I can go."

"That's six hours from now."

"That'll give me time for at least ten more kisses."

"Well, of course. What else would you do while someone is trying to kill you besides go out and tongue tango with as many strangers as possible?"

"They weren't trying to kill me, they were trying to abduct me. It's totally different. Come on, I want to do something fun. Something with boys."

"Or we could not do that."

"Look, just because you are a founding member of

Down with Fun Inc. doesn't mean that the rest of us want to sign up."

"I am not a founding member of Down with Fun Inc. I like fun. But—"

"Funkiller."

"—somehow the idea of wandering around while 'a ton of people' are trying to kidnap you, doesn't sound fun to me. It sounds like a good way to get into the *Guinness Book of World Records* under 'Plan, comma, World's Most Stupid.' Plus innocent bystanders could get caught in the middle when the ton of people find you."

"'If,' not 'when.' And they don't care about anyone but me."

Miranda rolled her eyes and turned back around. "That's why they're called innocent *by*standers. Because they were standing *by* you and accidentally got hurt."

"Then you should definitely get away from me. Seriously, although there's nothing I'd rather do than sit parked in a homeless person's bathroom for six hours with only you for company, I think it would be safer for both of us if I take my chances elsewhere. Like at that ice cream place we passed on the way here. Did you see the lips on the guy behind the counter? They were mythic. Drop me there and I'll be all set."

"You're so not going anywhere."

"Really? Because that sound you hear? Is me reaching for the door handle."

"Really? Because that sound *you* hear? Is me engaging the child lock."

In the rearview mirror, Miranda saw Sibby's eyes blaze.

"You're really mean," Sibby said. "Something horrible must have happened to you to make you so mean."

"I'm not mean. I'm just trying to keep you safe."

"Are you sure it's me you're thinking about? Not some skeleton in your closet? Like the time you—"

Miranda turned up the radio.

"Turn that down! I was talking and I'm the customer."

"Not anymore."

Sibby yelled really loud, "What happened to your sister?"

"I don't know what you are talking about," Miranda yelled back.

"That's a lie."

Miranda didn't say anything.

"I asked you before if you had a sister and you got all teary," Sibby shouted in her ear. "Why won't you tell me?"

Miranda turned down the radio. "Can you give me three good reasons why I should?"

"It might make you feel better. It would give us

something to talk about while we sit here. And if you don't tell me, I'm going to start guessing."

Miranda leaned her head back, checked her watch, and turned to stare out the window. "Be my guest."

"You bugged her so much she left? You bored her so much she left? Or did you drive her away with the huge stick you keep up your butt?"

"Stop being tender with my feelings. Go on, tell me what you really think."

From the backseat Sibby said, "That might have been too mean. Sorry."

Miranda didn't say anything.

"You don't really have a stick in your butt. You couldn't drive then, right? Ha-ha?"

Silence.

"But I mean, you started it. With the child-lock thing. I'm not a child. I'm fourteen."

More silence.

"I said I was sorry." In the backseat Sibby slumped, sighed. "Fine. Be that way."

Silence. Until, for no reason she could explain, Miranda said, "They died."

Sibby sat up quick now, leaning toward the front seat. "Who? Your sisters?"

"Everyone. My whole family."

"Was it because of something you did?"

"Yes. And because of something I didn't do. I think."

"Um, Grandma Grim, that doesn't make any sense. How can *not* doing something—wait, you *think*? Don't you know what happened?"

"I can't really remember anything from that part of my life."

"You mean from that day?"

"No. From that year. And the year after. Anything pretty much from when I was ten until when I turned twelve. And there are a few other holes, too."

"You mean that stuff is just too painful to remember?"

"No, it's just . . . gone. All I have are impressions." And the dreams. Really really bad dreams.

"Like what?"

"Like that I wasn't where I should have been and something happened and I let everyone down . . ." She stopped, waved a hand in the air.

"Wait, you actually think you could have stopped whatever happened to them? By yourself? When you were four years younger than me?"

Miranda's throat felt like it was closing up. She'd never told anyone even that much of her real history before, never talked about it, not even with Kenzi. Ever. She swallowed hard. "I could have tried. I could have been there and tried."

"Oh my gods, now this is some kind of pity party. Yawn. Wake me when you're done."

Miranda gaped at her in the mirror. "I told you I

didn't want to talk about it but you kept bugging me and now you turn into the mayor of TellItLikeItIsVille?" Swallowing again. "You little—"

"You don't even know what happened! How can you feel so bad about it? Plus, I don't see how that can be your fault. You weren't even there and you were only ten. I think you should stop obsessing about some mystery thing that is ancient history and live in the mo."

"I'm sorry, did you just tell me to 'live in the mo'?"

"Yes. You know, ditch the past and try focusing on what's going on in the present. Like that the song on the radio right now? Sucks. And that there is a whole city of cute boys out there I am not kissing." Miranda took a deep breath, but before she could say anything, Sibby went on. "I know, I know you say you're sorry to the people you knock out because you never got to say sorry to your family, and you have to keep me safe because you couldn't keep them safe. I get it now."

"That is *not* what's going on. I—"

"Blah blah blah, insert denials here. Anyway, why does 'safe' have to mean sitting in this car with you all night? Isn't there somewhere we could blend in? Instead of hiding? I'm good at blending. I'm like butter."

"Oh yeah, you're totally like butter. In fact, in your Madonna-called-and-she-wants-her-costume-from-the-'Borderline'-video-back outfit, you're practically invisible."

"Good one, Funkiller. Come on, let's go somewhere."

Miranda turned all the way around in her seat and said, "Let me sound it out for you. Someone. Is. Trying. To. Kill. You."

"No. They. Are. Not. You keep saying that, but I've told you. They can't kill me. You should really work on this obsession you have with people getting killed. And I have to be honest with you, I'm getting bored. What do you have the radio set to, K-CRAP? There is no way we are staying in this car for six hours."

Miranda had to agree with her. Because if they did, it was now clear she'd kill Sibby herself.

That's when she thought of the perfect place for them to go.

"You want to blend in?" she asked.

"Yes. With boys."

"Guys," Miranda said.

"What?"

"Normal American girls from this century call them guys, not boys. If you want to blend in."

For a second, Sibby looked shocked. Then she gave a little smile. "Oh. Yes. Guys."

"'Yeah,' not 'yes.' Unless you're talking to a grown-up."

"Yeah."

"And it's 'Oh my God' or 'God,' not 'gods.'"

"Did I—?"

"Yeah. And no one ever has or ever will say, 'live in the mo.'"

"Just wait."

"No. Never. Oh, and no paying guys for kisses. You don't need to. They should feel lucky to kiss you."

Sibby frowned. "Why are you being so nice to me and helping me? You don't even like me."

"Because I know what it's like to be far from home, alone, trying to fit in. And to never be able to tell anyone the truth about who you are."

After they'd been driving in silence for a few minutes, Sibby said, "Have you ever killed someone with your bare hands?"

Miranda looked at her in the rearview. "Not yet."

"Ha-ha."

8

"You're crazy," Sibby said as they walked in. Her eyes were pancake-size. "You said this would suck. This doesn't suck. This is fantastic."

Miranda shuddered. They'd snuck into the Grand Hall of the Santa Barbara Historical Society by an emergency exit that had been propped open so prom attendees could slip out to get stoned, and glancing around, Miranda could see how getting stoned would be super-appealing. The walls of the room had been covered in blue satin with white stars embroidered on it, the four big columns in the middle were draped in red and white ribbons, the tables off to the side were covered in American flag–print cloths with fishbowl centerpieces in which the fish had been somehow dyed red and blue, and around the edges major American landmarks such as Mount Rushmore, the White House, the Statue of Liberty, the Liberty Bell, and the Old Faithful geyser had been reconstructed—out of sugar cubes. Courtesy of Ariel West's father. Ariel had announced the previous day at assembly that after the prom all the decorations would be donated to "the poor hungry people of Santa Barbara who need sugar."

Miranda didn't know if it was that, the balloons on rubber cords hanging from the ceiling that bounced lazily up and down as people passed under them, or foreboding, but she had a distinct queasy feeling.

Sibby was in heaven.

"Remember—most of the guys here came with dates, so try to be subtle with the Kissing Bandit stuff," Miranda said.

"Yeah, fine."

"And if you hear me call to you, you come."

"Do I look like a dog to you?" Miranda gave her a sharp glance. Sibby said, "Fine, okay, Funkiller."

"And if you feel like anything weird is going on at all, you—"

"—let you know. I've got it. Now you go and have some fun yourself. Oh, right, you probably don't know how. Well, when in doubt, ask yourself, 'What Would Sibby Do?'"

"Can I unsubscribe from that list, please?"

Sibby was too busy scanning the room to respond.

"Whoa, who's that hot dinner in the corner over there?" she asked. "The guy in the glasses?"

Miranda looked around for a hot dinner but all she saw was Phil Emory. "His name is Phillip."

"Helllllo, Phillip," Sibby said, plotting a direct course for him.

Miranda stashed her skate bag underneath a table and stayed close to the wall, between the White House and Old Faithful, partially to keep Sibby in view and partially to avoid being noticed by any faculty members. She'd changed in the employee bathroom from her work suit into the only other thing she had with her, but although it was red, white, and blue, she didn't think that her Roller Derby uniform was really appropriate prom attire. There were two uniforms in her skate bag, a home uniform— white satin halter top and bottom with blue cape and red, white, and blue stripes on the skirt (if you could call something that was five inches long and required attached panties to be worn under it a skirt)—and an away uniform: the same thing, only in blue. She'd decided white was more formal, but she was pretty sure that wearing it with her black work flats was not helping the look.

She'd been standing there for a while, wondering how everyone but her was completely capable of being on a dance floor without debilitating anyone, when she heard a pair of heartbeats she recognized and saw Kenzi and Beth sliding through the crowd toward her.

"You came!" Kenzi said, giving her a big hug. One of the things Miranda loved about Kenzi was that she acted like she was on Ecstasy even when she wasn't, telling people that she loved them, hugging them, never embarrassed about it. "I'm so glad you're here. It didn't feel right without you. So, are you ready to unshackle yourself from the insecurities of your youth? Ready to own your future?"

Kenzi and Beth were dressed to own anything, Miranda thought. Kenzi was wearing a skin-tight blue backless dress and had gotten a black panther with a blue sapphire eye painted on her back. Beth was in a red satin minidress and had a gold snake bracelet with two ruby eyes wrapped around her upper arm (or at least Miranda assumed they were rubies since Beth's parents were two of the biggest movie stars in Bollywood). On them, adulthood looked like a totally cool and exciting party with an excellent DJ that you could only get into if you were on the VIP list.

Miranda glanced at her skating uniform. "I guess I should have known that when the time came to own my future I'd be dressed like a member of the Ice Capades B-squad."

"No way, you look fantastic," Beth said, and Miranda would have assumed she was being sarcastic except that Beth was one of those people who was born without sarcasm.

"Truly," Kenzi confirmed. "You're deep in H2T territory." H2T stood for Hot to Trot. "I see great things for your adulthood."

"And I see a visit to the eye doctor for you," Miranda prophesied. In the distance Miranda saw Sibby pull Phillip Emory onto the dance floor.

Miranda turned back to Kenzi. "Do you think I'm a fun person? Am I a Grandma Grim? A funkiller?"

"Grandma Grim? Fun*killer*?" Kenzi repeated. "What are you talking about? Did you hit your head at derby practice again?"

"No, I'm serious. Am I fun?"

"Yes," Kenzi said solemnly.

"Yes," Beth agreed.

"Except when you get all MLAS," Kenzi modified. "And when you have your period. And around your birthday. Oh, there was that one time—"

"Forget it." Miranda's eyes drifted to Sibby, who now appeared to be leading a conga line.

"I'm kidding," Kenzi said, turning Miranda's face from the dance floor to hers. "Yes, I think you are really fun. I mean, who else would dress up as Magnum P.I. for Halloween?"

"Or think of entertaining the kids on the cancer ward by reenacting *Dawson's Creek* with Precious Moments figurines?" Beth added.

Kenzi nodded. "That's right. Even children battling

cancer think you're fun. And they're not the only ones."

Something about Kenzi's tone when she said the last part made Miranda worried. "What did you do?"

"She was brilliant," Beth said.

Now Miranda was even more scared. "Tell me."

"It was nothing, just some research," Kenzi said

"What kind of research?" For the first time Miranda noticed that there was writing up the length of Kenzi's arm.

Kenzi said, "About Will and Ariel. They're totally not going out."

"You *asked* him?"

"It's called an interview," Kenzi said.

"No. Oh no. Tell me you're kidding." Sometimes having a roommate who wanted to be a journalist was dangerous.

"Relax, he didn't suspect a thing. I made it seem like I was making small talk," Kenzi said.

"She was great," Beth confirmed.

Miranda started wishing for trapdoors again.

"Anyway, I asked him why he thought Ariel asked him to the prom and he said"—here Kenzi consulted her arm—"'To make someone else jealous.' So of course I asked who and he went, 'Anyone. That's what Ariel thrives on, other people's jealousy.' Isn't that perceptive? Especially for a guy?"

"He's smart," Beth put in. "And nice."

Miranda nodded absently, looking for Sibby on the dance floor. At first she didn't see her but then she spotted her in a dark corner with Phillip. Talking, not kissing. For some reason that made her smile.

"Look, we made her happy!" Kenzi said, and she sounded so genuinely pleased that Miranda didn't want to tell her the truth.

"Thanks for finding all that out," Miranda said. "It's—"

"You haven't even heard the best part," Kenzi said. "I asked why he agreed to go to prom with Ariel if they're not a couple and he said"—glancing at her arm—"'Because no one made me a better offer.'"

Beth reminded her, "With that cute smile."

"Right, with cute smile. And he looked directly at me when he said it and he was so clearly talking about you!"

"Clearly." Miranda loved her friends even if they were delusional.

"Stop gazing at me like I've been one-stop shopping at the Lobotomy Store, Miranda," Kenzi said. "I'm completely right. He likes you and he's not taken. Stop thinking and grab him. Go live ITM."

"ITM?"

"In the Mo," Beth elaborated.

Miranda gaped. "No. Way."

"What?" Kenzi asked.

"Nothing." Miranda shook her head. "Even if he's

single, what makes you think Will wants to go out with *me*?"

Kenzi squinted at her. "Um, breezing past all the sappy stuff about how you're nice and smart I have to say because I'm your best friend, have you looked in the mirror recently?"

"Ha-ha. Trust me—"

"Bye!" Beth said, interrupting her and dragging Kenzi away. "See you later!"

"Don't forget! ITM!" Kenzi added over her shoulder. "Drink a can of man!"

"Where are you—" Miranda started to say, then heard a heartbeat close behind her and swung around.

Nearly banging her shoulder against Will's chest.

9

HE SAID, "HI."

And she said, "Ho." God. GOD. Could she just say one normal thing? Thanks Crazy Mouth.

He cocked an eyebrow at her. "I didn't know you were coming to prom."

"I—changed my mind at the last minute."

"You look nice."

"You too." Which was an understatement. He looked like a double stack of cinnamon apple pancakes with a side order of bacon and hash browns (extra crispy). Like the best thing Miranda had ever laid eyes on.

She felt herself staring at him, then looked away, blushing. There was a moment of silence. Another one. Don't let it go beyond four seconds, she reminded herself. It had to have been one second already; that left three, now two, say something! Say—

"Are you wearing space pants?" Miranda asked him.

"What?"

How did it end? Oh, right. She said, "Because your butt is fine."

He gazed at her in that way he had like he was measuring her for a straitjacket. "I think—" he started, then stopped and seemed to be having trouble talking. Cleared his throat three times before finally saying, "I think the line is 'because your butt is out of this world.'"

"Oh. That makes a lot more sense. I can see that. See, I read it in this book about how to get guys to like you and they said it was a line that never failed but I got interrupted in the middle and the line before it was about china—not the country, the kind you eat off of—and that is where the fine part was but I must have gotten them confused." He just kept staring at her. She remembered the other advice from the book, "when in doubt, make an offer," reached out, grabbed the first thing she could put her hand on, held it up to his chin, and said, "Nuts?"

He looked like he was about to choke. He cleared his throat a few times, took the nuts from her, put the bowl back on the table, stepped toward her so that their noses were almost touching, and said, "You read a book about this?"

Miranda couldn't even hear his heartbeat over the

sound of her own. "Yes, I did. Because clearly I wasn't doing it right. I mean, if you kiss a guy and he pulls away from you and looks at you like your skin just turned to purple slime, clearly you need to spend some time at the self-help section of—"

"You talk more when you're nervous," he said, still standing close to her.

"No I don't. That's absurd. I'm just trying to explain to you—"

"Do I make you nervous?"

"No. I'm not nervous."

"You're trembling."

"I'm cold. I'm wearing practically zero clothes."

His glance went to her lips, then back to her eyes. "I noticed."

Miranda gulped. "Look, I should—"

He caught her wrist before she could take off. "That kiss you gave me was the hottest kiss I've ever had. I pulled away because I was afraid I wouldn't be able to stop myself from ripping off your clothes. And that didn't seem like the right way to end a first date. I didn't want you to think that was all I was interested in."

She stared at him. There was silence again, but this time she didn't worry about how long it went on.

"Why didn't you tell me?" she said finally.

"I tried to, but every time I saw you afterward you disappeared. I got the feeling you were avoiding me."

"I didn't want things to be awkward."

"Yeah, there was nothing awkward about you hiding behind a plant when I came into the dining hall at lunch on Wednesday."

"I wasn't hiding. I was, um, breathing. You know, oxygen. From the plant. Very oxygenated, that air is."

Insert head in oven now.

"Of course. I should have thought of that."

"It's a health thing. Not many people know about it."

Leave until no longer HALF BAKED.

"No, I'm sure they—"

Miranda blurted. "Did you really mean that? About liking it when I kissed you?"

"I really did. A lot."

Her hands were shaking. She reached up and pulled him toward her.

Just as the music went off, the emergency-exit lighting went on and a tinny voice announced over a loudspeaker, "Please make your way to the nearest exit and leave the building immediately."

She and Will were pushed in different directions by the crowd surging to the door, being guided by four men in full body armor. The message kept repeating, but Miranda wasn't hearing it or Ariel West screaming that someone was going to *PAY* for *RUINING* her *NIGHT* or the person saying that dude, this was the sweetest way to end a prom ever, man, he was so high. She was hearing again the one-two-three cha-cha heartbeat of Deputy Reynolds, slightly muffled by body armor. This was no drill.

"It's us, isn't it?" Sibby said, rushing over to stand next to Miranda. "That's why those storm-trooper guys are here. For us."

"Yeah."

"You were right. I should have stayed hidden. This is my fault. I don't want anyone to get hurt. I'll just turn myself over to these people, and they'll have to let—"

Miranda interrupted her. "After all that? With only three hours left to go? And you, blend-it-like-butter girl? No way. It's not over. We can totally get out of this."

She tried to sound confident, but she was terrified. *Just what do you think you're doing?* U-Suck channel demanded.

I have no idea.

Sibby looked at her, eyes blazing with hope. "Do you mean it? You have a way out?"

Miranda swallowed, took a deep breath, and said to Sibby, "Follow me." To herself: *Please don't fail.*

10

*I*T WORKED PERFECTLY.

Almost. There were six guards blocking the exits and another four at the door, checking everyone as they left. Ten total. All in body armor and masks, explaining patiently that there had been a bomb threat and it was important to evacuate as quickly as possible. No one questioned why they were armed with the automatic weapons they kept using to push the crowd along.

No one except Dr. Trope, who went up to one of them and said, "Young man, I ask you to keep your weapons away from my students," distracting him just long enough for Miranda and Sibby to get swallowed into the middle of the crowd.

They'd navigated by the first two storm troopers, with only two left when Ariel yelled, "Dr. Trope? Dr.

Trope? Look, there she is, Miranda Kiss. I told you she crashed the prom. She's right there in the middle. You have to—"

Four men with automatic weapons suddenly swiveled and waded into the mass of students. Miranda whispered, "Duck," to Sibby and the two of them bobbed beneath the surface of the crowd, crawling back into the Great Hall.

Behind her she heard Dr. Trope saying, "Where is she? Where did she go? I'm not leaving one of my pupils in there." And the storm trooper saying, "Please, sir, you need to evacuate. We'll find her. Rest assured."

Miranda decided that if she got out of this alive, she'd be a lot nicer to Dr. Trope. *If.*

She dragged Sibby over to Old Faithful and said, "In there. Now."

"Why can't I hide in the White House? Why does it have to be in the volcano?"

"I might need part of the White House. Please, just do it. They won't be able to make you out if they have night goggles."

"What about you? You're wearing white."

"I match the decorations."

"Wow, you're really good at this. This planning stuff. How'd you learn how to—"

Miranda was wondering the same thing. Wondering why as soon as she'd heard the announcement some part of her brain had started measuring her distance to the exits, looking around for weapons, watching the door. Her senses going into overdrive was a relief; it meant some of her powers were cooperating. But did she have the strength to take on ten armed men? The most she'd ever taken on at one time before was three, and they hadn't been toting machine guns. She'd have to be crafty rather than direct. She said to Sibby, "Give me your boots."

"For what?"

"To get rid of some of our competition so we can get out of here."

"But I really like these—"

"Give them to me. And also a rubber bracelet."

Miranda set her trap, then held her breath as a guard approached. She heard him say into the walkie-talkie, "Southwest pillar. I've got one," and saw the ribbons stir as he used the butt of his gun to push them aside.

Heard him say, "What the—"

And fired George Washington's sugar nose at him with the slingshot she'd made out of Sibby's rubber bracelet and a fork. All her target work paid off because it hit him at exactly the right point to send him plunging forward. He went down headfirst just hard enough to be disoriented and docile while she tied his hands and feet with the ribbons from the pillar. "I'm really sorry," she said, flipping him over to gag him with a piece of dinner roll, then smiled. "Oh, hi, Craig. Not your day, is it? I hope your head's feeling better. What? It's not? It will. Try rubbing some insta-hot on your wrists and ankles when they untie you. Bye."

She'd just grabbed the boots she'd used at the base of the column as a decoy when she heard another guard coming fast from her left. She threw a boot at him Frisbee style and heard a satisfying *swack* as he fell down, too.

Two down, eight to go.

She was apologizing to the one she'd hit with the shoe, who was out cold—it was nice to know ankle boots were good for something—when the walkie-talkie on his belt came to life. "Leon, this is the Gardener. Where are you? State your position. Copy?"

Miranda picked up the unconscious guard's walkie-talkie and said into it, "I thought your name was Caleb Reynolds, Deputy. Why the Gardener stuff? Or, as my friend likes to call you, Plant Boy."

A crackle. Then Deputy Reynolds's voice through the walkie-talkie. "Miranda? Is that you? Where are you? Miranda?"

"Right here," she whispered in his ear. She'd snuck up behind him, and now as he turned, her arm came around his neck with the heel of the boot pointed at his throat.

"What are you stabbing me with?" he asked.

"All you need to know is that it's going to cause you a lot of pain and probably a bad infection if you don't start telling me how many people there are here and what their plan is."

"There are ten in here, five more watching the exits outside. But I'm on your side."

"Really, Gardener? That's not how it looked at the house."

"You didn't give me a chance to talk to the girl."

"You're going to have to do better than that. I'm not a mix tape, you can't play me."

"Do you have any idea what she is?"

"*What* she is? Not really."

His heart rate sped up now. "She's a real-life flesh-and-blood prophet. The Cumean Sibyl. She's one of ten people who between them supposedly know and can control the whole future of the world."

"Wow. I thought she was just an annoying fourteen-year-old with wild hormones."

"The Sibyl operates through different bodies. Or that's what they think. These people I'm working with. Wack jobs. They pretend they want to protect her, keep her prophecies from being exploited by the unscrupulous, but I think they're actually into extortion. I heard one of them say they could ransom the girl for eight figures." His heart rate slowed as he talked. "My job was to find out where she was supposed to be picked up, so they could send someone there with some trinket of hers to show we had her, and get the Overseer to pay up."

Miranda didn't like the sound of the word *trinket* at all. "But you weren't going to?"

"They're just using this religion stuff as a cover for their greed. It's disgusting. I'm all set to stop them, and then you"—getting agitated, his heartbeat spiking— "you come along in the middle and mess it up."

Miranda knew he was genuinely angry. "Stop them how?"

"I was supposed to be getting the location of her pickup place from her, right? When you crashed in, I was going to tell her what to say, a place I'd picked out with the task force, then when the wackos went there, they'd be picked up by the police. Meanwhile I'd get the Sibyl safely to the real rendezvous. But you come in and blow it. Months of police work down the tubes." His heartbeat was slow and even again.

Miranda let him go. "I'm so sorry," she said.

He turned to scowl at her, changing it to a half smile when he saw what she was wearing. "Nice look on you." He paused for a second, then said, "You know, there's a way we could still make this work. Do you have another outfit like that?"

"My skating uniform? Yeah. But it's not the same color. It's more blue."

"That doesn't matter as long as it's close. With you

two dressed as twins we'll be able to fool them into thinking that you're the Sibyl, use you as a decoy while we sneak her out to safety."

Talking quickly, he outlined the rest of his plan. Miranda said, "It would be better if we wore the wigs and masks, too. To complete the disguise."

"That's right. Perfect. Go toward the employee entrance, the one you used to sneak in. There's someone guarding the outer door but there's a door on the left that is clear. It goes to an office. I'll deal with these guys and then come—"

He stopped talking, lifted his gun, and fired behind her. Turning, Miranda saw he'd shot one of the guards.

"He saw us together," he told her. "I couldn't let one of those bastards get you or tell the others. I'll distract them, keep them over here. You get the Sibyl, change, and wait for me in the office."

She was already moving away when she paused and said, "How did you find us?"

His heartbeat slowed. "Put out a bulletin on your car."

"I should have thought of that," Miranda said, then took off as he radioed, "Man down—man down."

Sibby was frantic when Miranda got back to her. "What happened? Did you get shot?"

"No. I got us a ride out of here."

"How?"

Miranda explained as they changed, then skirted the edges of the Great Hall toward the director's office. As they moved, she heard Deputy Reynolds barking orders to the guards, keeping them busy in other parts of the room, saying at one point, "No, don't turn on the lights—that will give them an advantage!" At another, heard a grunt of pain that sounded like someone being knocked out. She was impressed.

They reached the director's office without running into anyone. Sibby sat in the desk chair. Miranda was pacing, walking back and forth to the ticktock of the big clock on the director's mantelpiece, picking up and putting down objects, a crystal bowl, a box of stationery, weighing them in her hand. A family picture of a man, woman, two small boys, a dog sitting together at the edge of a pier with the sun setting behind them. The dog was wearing someone's hat, a real full member of the family.

A hand came down in front of the picture. "Hello, Miranda? I was asking you something?"

Miranda put the picture down. "Sorry. What?"

"How do you know you're right about him?"

"I just do. Trust me."

"But if you're wrong—"

"I'm not."

The clock ticked. Miranda paced. Sibby said, "I hate that clock."

Tick. Pace. Sibby: "I'm not sure I can do this."

Miranda stopped and looked at her. "Of course you can."

"I'm not brave like you."

"Excuse me? The girl who got—how many guys is it now? Twenty-three?"

"Twenty-four."

"Twenty-four guys to kiss her? You're brave." Miranda hesitated. "Know how many guys I've kissed?"

"How many?"

"Three."

Sibby gaped at her, burst out laughing. "Gods, no wonder you're so repressed. This had better work or you'll have had one seriously sad life."

"Thanks."

11

*E*IGHTEEN MINUTES LATER, DEPUTY Sergeant Caleb
Reynolds stood outside the door of the director's
office, watching them through a crack. It had taken him
slightly longer than expected to get everything in place,
but he felt good, confident, about how it was all going to
play out. Especially now seeing the two girls in the Bee's
Roller Derby outfits, tight little skirts and tops, even had
the wigs and masks on. They were identical except one
of them was in blue, the other in white. Like little dolls,
yeah, he liked to think of them that way. His little dolls.

Expensive dolls.

The blue doll saying, "Are you sure the fact that you
want to kiss him isn't getting in the way of your judgment, Miranda?"

And the white doll saying, "Who says I want to kiss

him? You're the Kissing Bandit."

"Who says I want to kiss him?" the blue doll mimicked. "Please. You should really learn to have some fun. Live in the mo."

"Maybe I will as soon as I get rid of you, Sibby."

The blue doll stuck out her tongue, almost making him laugh. They were cute together, these two. Blue doll said, "I'm serious. How do you know we can trust him?"

"He has his own agenda," the white doll explained, "and it works with ours."

Then he really did have to stifle a laugh. She had no idea how correct she was. About that first part.

And how wrong about the second.

He pushed the door open and saw them both turn to him with you-are-my-hero expressions in their eyes.

"Are you ready, Miss Cumean?"

Blue doll nodded.

His little white doll saying now, "Take good care of her. You know how important she is."

"I will. I'll get her settled and come back for the second part of the operation. Don't open the door for anyone but me."

"Right."

He was back less than a minute later.

"Was everything okay? Is Sibby safe?"

"It went perfectly. My men were exactly in position. It could not have gone smoother."

"Okay, so how long do we wait before I run out?"

He walked toward her, backing her against the wall. He said, "There's been a change of plans."

"What, you've added a part where you kiss me? Before the part where I pretend to be Sibby and lead the guards into the SWAT-team trap?"

He liked the way she smiled when she said it. He reached up to caress her cheek and said, "Not exactly, Miranda." His hands slid from her face to her neck.

"What are you tal—"

Before she could finish, she was pressed against the wall, hanging a foot above the ground, his hands around her throat. He tightened them slightly as he said, "It's just you and me now. I know all about you. Who you are. What you can do."

"Really?" she choked out.

"Yes, really. *Princess.*" He saw her eyes get wide and felt her swallow hard. "I knew that would get your attention."

"I don't know what you're talking about."

"I know about the bounty on your head. Miranda Kiss wanted, alive or dead. My original plan had been to leave you alive for a while, bring you in after a few weeks, but unfortunately you just had to interfere. Should have minded your own business instead of mine, Princess. Now I can't run the risk of your getting in the way."

"You mean in the way of what you're doing with

Sibby? So you were the one who wanted the money. You betrayed those others and made them think you were part of their cause, just like you betrayed us."

"Such a smart girl."

"You kill me, kidnap her, and collect money? Is that it?"

"Yep. Just like Monopoly, Princess. Pass go, collect two hundred dollars. Only in this case it's more like fifty million. For the girl."

"Wow." She looked genuinely impressed. "And how much do you get for me?"

"Dead? Five million. You're worth more alive; apparently some people think you're some teen Wonder Woman, have superpowers. But I can't take the chance."

"You already said that," she rasped.

"What, are you bored, Miranda?" He tightened his grip a little. "Sorry this wasn't more of a storybook ending," he said, smiling at her, holding her eyes with his own as he choked her.

He could tell she was struggling to breathe now. "If you're going to kill me, can't you just get on with it? This is kind of uncomfortable."

"What, my hands? Or the feeling that you're a failure—"

"I'm not a failure."

"—again."

She spit in his face.

"Still got some fire. I really admire that about you. I think you and I could have gotten along nicely. Unfortunately, there just isn't time."

She gave one last fight, clawing at him with all her remaining strength. It was inspiring how hard she worked. Finally her little fists fell hopelessly to her sides.

He leaned in close to her face. "Any last words?"

"Three: Listerine breath strips. You really need them."

He laughed, then tightened the hands around her neck until they overlapped. "Good-bye."

For a second, his eyes burned into hers. Then there was a sharp crack and something heavy came down on his head from behind. He staggered forward, his hands letting go of the girl as he fell to the ground unconscious.

He never knew what hit him, the blue doll thought, still gripping the clock she'd used to knock him out. Or who.

12

MIRANDA, DRESSED IN THE blue uniform, pushed aside the man she'd just hit over the head with the clock to reach Sibby. She still had handcuff bracelets around her wrists, each dangling a piece of chain. Her wrists, her hands, were shaking.

She lifted the unconscious girl gently. "Sibby, come on, open your eyes."

It wasn't supposed to have taken so long. The plan had been simple: She and Sibby would switch identities by switching outfits. When Deputy Reynolds double-crossed them, like Miranda knew he would, it would be Miranda disguised as Sibby he'd hand over to his crew, and she'd deal with them, then come back and rescue Sibby.

At least, that's how it should have gone.

"Okay, Sib, time to wake up," Miranda said, carrying the girl now, cradling her pressed against her chest as she moved as quickly as possible. She could hear Sibby's heartbeat, but it was faint, and slow. Getting fainter. *This is not happening.*

"Rise and shine, Sibby," she said, her voice cracking. "Up and at 'em."

Miranda hadn't expected to find all five of Deputy Reynolds's goons waiting for her—shouldn't someone have been in the getaway car?—and especially hadn't anticipated the woman he'd picked up from the airport having rhinestone-studded brass knuckles. The blow to the head had given them time to cuff Miranda to a pipe and made her a little weak, so it had taken her longer than it should have to knock them off with a series of roundhouse kicks and one side scissor, then break the chain on the cuffs and free herself. Giving Deputy Reynolds more time with Sibby's esophagus than she'd planned.

A lot more.

The heartbeat was getting softer, harder to hear.

"I'm so sorry, Sibby. I should have gotten here sooner. I tried my best, but I couldn't get the handcuffs off and I was too weak and I failed and—" Miranda was having trouble seeing and realized she was crying. She stumbled but kept running. "Sibby, you've got to be okay. You can't go. If you don't come back, I swear I'll never have fun again. Not once." The heartbeat was just a whisper now, the girl in her arms a pale ghost. Miranda choked back a sob. "God, Sibby, *please*—"

Sibby's eyes flickered. Color surged into her cheeks and her heart picked up. "Did it work?" she whispered.

Miranda swallowed the huge lump in her throat and resisted the urge to crush her. "It worked."

"Did you—"

"Clocked him with the clock, as requested."

Sibby smiled, reached her hand up to Miranda's cheek, then closed her eyes again. They didn't reopen until they were in the car with the historical society behind them. She sat up and looked around. "I'm in the front seat."

"Special occasion," Miranda explained. "Don't get used to it."

"Right." Sibby worked her neck back and forth. "That was a good plan. Trading outfits so they'd think you were me and not worry so much about restraints."

"They still went all out." Miranda pushed the cape back. "I broke the chain, but I can't get the bracelets off." Thinking for some reason of Kenzi at the prom saying, *Are you ready to unshackle yourself from the insecurities of your youth? Are you ready to own your future?*

"What happened to Plant Boy?"

"I called in an anonymous tip telling them where to find him and the bodies of the guards he shot. He should be on his way to jail."

"How did you know you were right? That he was trying to trick us?"

"I can tell when people are lying."

"How?"

"Different things. Little gestures. Mostly by listening to their heartbeats."

"Like if they speed up, they're lying?"

"Everyone is different. You need to know how they react when they're telling the truth to know how they react when they're lying. His heartbeat gets slower, more even when he lies, like he's trying to be extra careful."

Sibby looked at her more closely. "You can hear people's *heartbeats*?"

"I hear a lot of things."

Sibby took that in. "When Plant Boy was strangling me because he thought I was you? He called me Princess. And said some people thought you had superpowers like a teen Wonder Woman or something."

Miranda felt her chest get tight. "He did?"

"And he said there was a bounty on your head. Alive or dead. Although I'm sorry to say that I'm worth ten times as much as you are."

"It's not nice to brag."

"Is it true? That you're Wonder Woman?"

"Maybe the lack of oxygen went to your head but Wonder Woman is a comic-book character. Made up.

I'm a real, normal person."

Sibby snorted. "You are definitely not normal. You're *totally* neurotic." A pause. "That wasn't an answer. Are you really a princess with superpowers?"

"Are you really a sacred prophet who knows everything that is going to happen?"

Their eyes met. Neither of them said anything.

Sibby stretched, sprawling out over the front seat, and Miranda turned up the radio and they drove on in silence, both of them smiling.

After a few miles Sibby said, "I'm starving. Could we stop for a burger?"

"Yeah, but we're on a schedule, so no kissing strange guys."

"I knew you were going to say that."

13

MIRANDA SAT IN THE car watching the power boat disappear on the horizon, taking Sibby wherever she was going. *You have no time to relax,* she reminded herself. *Deputy Reynolds might be headed for prison, but he can still talk, and you know he lied about how he found you, which means someone at Chatsworth knows something, and then there's the question of who put the bounty on your head and—*

Her cell phone rang. She reached across the seat to grab her suit jacket and tried to jam her hand into the pocket to get the phone, but the handcuff bracelet kept getting caught. She turned the jacket over and dumped everything onto her lap.

She caught it on the last ring. "Hello."

"Miranda? It's Will."

Her heart stopped. "Hi." Suddenly feeling shy. "Did you, um, have fun at prom?"

"Parts of it. You?"

"Me too. Parts of it."

"I looked for you after the bomb threat, but I didn't see you."

"Yeah, it got kind of hectic."

There was a pause and they both started talking at once. He said, "You first," and she said, "No, you," and they both cracked up and he started, "Listen, I don't know if you were planning to come to Sean's place for the after-party. Everyone is here. It's fun and all. But—"

"But?"

"I was wondering if maybe you'd want to get breakfast instead. At the Waffle House? Just the two of us?"

Miranda forgot to breathe. She said, "That would be completely fantastic." And remembering she wasn't supposed to be too eager, added, "I mean, that would be okay, I guess."

Will laughed, his warm-butter-melting-on-breakfast-treats laugh, and said, "I think it would be completely fantastic, too."

She hung up and saw that her hands were shaking. She was having breakfast with a guy. Not just a guy. With Will. A guy who wore space pants. And thought she was hot.

And possibly crazy. Which, p.s., accessorizing with

handcuffs is not exactly going to help.

She tried again to snap the bracelets with her hand but she couldn't. Either these weren't normal cuffs or knocking out ten people in one night—actually eight, since she'd done two of them twice—was the limit of her strength. Which was interesting, her strength having limits. She had a lot to learn about her powers. Later.

Right now, she had half an hour to find some other way to get the cuffs off. She started shoving things from her lap back into the pocket of her suit jacket so she could drive, then stopped when she saw an unfamiliar box.

It was the one Sibby had given her when they met— could it seriously be only eight hours ago? What had she said, something odd. Miranda remembered it now, Sibby handing her the name sign and the box and saying, "This must be yours." But with the emphasis different. "This *must* be yours."

Miranda opened the box. Inside, nestled in black velvet, was a handcuff key.

Are you ready to own your future?

It was worth a try.

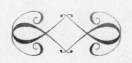

Hell
on
Earth

STEPHENIE MEYER

*G*ABE STARED ACROSS THE dance floor and frowned. He wasn't sure why he'd asked Celeste to the prom, and it was another mystery why she'd said yes. Even more mysterious now, watching her grip Heath McKenzie around the neck so tightly that Heath was probably having trouble breathing. Their bodies flattened into an indivisible mass as they swayed against the beat, ignoring the rhythm of the song thudding through the room. Heath's hands roamed over Celeste's glistening white dress in an intimate way.

"Tough luck, Gabe."

Gabe looked away from the spectacle his date was making to his approaching friend.

"Hey, Bry. Having a nice night?"

"Better than you, man, better than you," Bryan

answered, grinning. He lifted his cup of bilious green punch as if for a toast. Gabe touched his bottled water to Bryan's cup and sighed.

"I had no idea Celeste had a thing for Heath. What is he, her ex or something?"

Bryan took a gulp of the sinister-looking drink, made a face, and shook his head. "Not that I know of. I've never seen them even speak to each other before tonight."

Both of them stared at Celeste, who had apparently lost something she needed deep inside Heath's mouth.

"Huh," Gabe said.

"It's probably just the punch," Bryan said in an attempt to be encouraging. "I don't know how many people spiked it, but *ouch*. She might not even know that's not you out there."

Bryan took another swig and made another face.

"Why are you drinking that?" Gabe wondered aloud.

Bryan shrugged. "I don't know. Maybe the music will start to sound a little less pathetic after I force a glass of this down."

Gabe nodded. "My ears may never forgive me. I should have brought my iPod."

"I wonder where Clara is. Is there some kind of girl-law that demands they spend a certain percentage of every event in the bathroom together?"

"Yes. Stiff penalties for girls who don't meet the quota."

Bryan laughed once, but then his smile faded and he fiddled with his bow tie for a moment. "About Clara . . . ," he began.

"You don't have to say anything," Gabe assured him. "She's an amazing girl. *And* you two are perfect for each other. I would've had to be blind not to see that."

"You really don't mind?"

"I told you to ask her to the prom, didn't I?"

"Yeah, you did. Sir Galahad makes another match. Seriously, man, do you ever think about yourself?"

"Sure, every hour on the hour. And hey, speaking of Clara . . . she better have a great time tonight or I'm going to break your nose." Gabe grinned a wide grin. "She and I are still good friends—don't think I won't call her to check."

Bryan rolled his eyes, but suddenly found it a little difficult to swallow. If Gabe Christensen wanted to break his nose, he wouldn't have much of a problem doing it—Gabe didn't mind getting his knuckles bruised or his permanent record blemished if it meant righting something that was wrong in his eyes.

"I'll take care of Clara," Bryan said, wishing that the words didn't sound so much like a vow. There was something about Gabe and his piercing blue eyes that made you feel that way—like doing the best you could at any given task. It got irritating sometimes. With a grimace, Bryan dumped the rest of his punch into the dead moss at the base of a fake ficus tree. "If she ever leaves the bathroom."

"Good man," Gabe said approvingly, but his smile twisted down on one side. Celeste and Heath had disappeared into the crowd.

Gabe wasn't sure what the protocol was when you got dumped at the prom. How was he supposed to make sure she got home safe? Was that Heath's job now?

Gabe wondered again why he'd asked Celeste to this dance.

She was a very pretty girl—pageant pretty. Perfect blond hair—so full it was fluffy—wide-spaced brown eyes, and curvy lips always painted a flattering shade of pink. Her lips weren't the only things that were curvy. She'd all but shut his brain down with the thin, clingy dress she'd worn tonight.

Her looks weren't the reason he'd noticed her, though. That reason was something else entirely.

It was stupid and embarrassing, really. Gabe would never, ever tell anyone else about this, but every now and then, he got this weird sense that someone needed help. Needed *him*. He'd gotten that inexplicable pull from Celeste, as if the shapely blonde was hiding a damsel in distress somewhere behind her flawless makeup.

Very stupid. And obviously wrong. Celeste didn't seem interested in any help from Gabe right now.

He scanned the dance floor again but couldn't pick her golden hair out of the crowd. He sighed.

"Hey, Bry, did you miss me?" Clara, her dark curly hair full of glitter, bounced free from a herd of females and joined them against the wall. The rest of the herd dispersed. "Hey, Gabe. Where's Celeste?"

Bryan put his arm around her shoulders. "I thought you left. Guess I'll have to cancel the hot plans I just made with—"

Clara's elbow caught Bryan in the solar plexus.

"Mrs. Finkle," Bryan continued, gasping the words and nodding toward the vice principal glaring from the corner of the room farthest away from the speakers. "We were going to sort failure notices by candlelight."

"Well, I wouldn't want you to miss that! I think I saw Coach Lauder by the cookies. Maybe I could talk him into some extra-credit pull-ups."

"Or maybe we could just dance," Bryan suggested.

"Sure, I can settle for that."

Laughing, they pressed their way toward the dance floor, Bryan's hands winding around Clara's waist.

Gabe was glad Clara hadn't waited for an answer to her question. It was a little embarrassing that he didn't have one.

"Hey, Gabe, where's Celeste?"

Gabe grimaced and turned to the sound of Logan's voice.

Logan was also solo for the moment. Perhaps it was his date's turn to exhibit girl-herding behavior.

"I couldn't say," Gabe admitted. "Have you seen her?"

Logan pursed his full lips for a minute, as if debating whether or not to say something. He ran a hand nervously across his springy black hair. "Well, I thought I did. I'm not exactly sure, though. . . . She's wearing a white dress, right?"

"Yeah—where is she?"

"I think I saw her in the lobby. Can't be positive. Her face was sort of hard to see. . . . David Alvarado's face was all over it. . . ."

"David Alvarado?" Gabe repeated in surprise. "Not Heath McKenzie?"

"Heath? Naw. It was definitely David."

Heath was a linebacker, blond and fair. David barely cleared five feet; his coloring was olive and his hair was black. No way to confuse the two.

Logan shook his head sadly. "Sorry, Gabe. That sucks."

"Don't worry about it."

"At least you're not in the stag boat alone," Logan said forlornly.

"Really? What happened to your date?"

Logan shrugged. "She's around here somewhere,

glowering at everyone. She doesn't want to dance, she doesn't want to talk, she doesn't want punch, she doesn't want to take pictures, and she doesn't want my company." He ticked each negative off on his fingers. "I don't know why she asked me in the first place. Probably just wanted to show off her dress—it *is* hot, I'll give her that. But she doesn't seem to care about showing anything now . . . Wish I'd asked someone else." Logan's eyes lingered wistfully on a group of girls fast dancing in a male-free circle. Gabe thought he saw Logan focus on one girl in particular.

"Why didn't you ask Libby?"

Logan sighed. "I don't know. I think . . . I think she would have liked it if I'd asked her, though. Oh well."

"Who's your date?"

"That new girl, Sheba. She's a little intense but really gorgeous, kinda exotic. I was too shocked to say anything but yes when she asked me to go with her. I thought that she, well, that she might be . . . fun . . . ," Logan finished lamely. What he'd really thought when Sheba had all but commanded him to take her to prom didn't seem entirely appropriate to be spoken aloud, especially to Gabe; lots of things seemed inappropriate around Gabe. It was just the opposite with Sheba. When he'd gotten a look at her mind-blowing red leather dress, his head had been full of ideas that somehow didn't feel in the least bit inappropriate while her deep, dark eyes had been focused on him.

"I don't think I've met her," Gabe said, interrupting Logan's brief fantasy.

"You'd remember if you had." Although Sheba had forgotten Logan quickly enough once they were in the door, hadn't she? "Hey, do you think maybe Libby came alone? I didn't hear about anyone asking her. . . ."

"Er, she came with Dylan."

"Oh," Logan said, crestfallen. Then he half-smiled. "Night's bad enough without getting tortured on top of everything else—weren't they supposed to have a band? This DJ . . ."

"I know. It's as if we're being punished for our sins," Gabe said with a laugh.

"Sins? Like you have any, Galahad the Pure."

"Are you kidding? I barely got off suspension in time to be allowed to come tonight." Of course, at the moment Gabe was wishing the timing hadn't been so helpful. "I'm lucky I didn't get expelled."

"Mr. Reese had it coming. Everyone knows that."

"Yeah, he did," Gabe said, a sudden edge sharpening his tone. Everyone at school was wary of Mr. Reese, but there wasn't much they could do until the math teacher crossed a line he shouldn't have. All the upperclassmen knew about Mr. Reese, too, but Gabe wasn't about to stand by while he stalked that clueless freshman kid. . . . Still, knocking out a teacher was a bit extreme. There was probably some better way to have handled the situation. His parents had been supportive, though, as usual.

Logan interrupted his thoughts. "Maybe we should take off," Logan said.

"I'd feel bad—if Celeste needs a way home . . ."

"That girl is *not* your type, Gabe." *She's pure evil—and a full-on whore,* Logan could have added, but those just weren't the kinds of things you wanted to say about any girl while Gabe was in hearing range. "Let her get a ride with the guy sticking his tongue down her throat."

Gabe sighed and shook his head. "I'll wait to make sure she's okay."

Logan groaned. "I can't believe you asked her. Well, can we ditch out long enough to pick up a few decent CDs at least? Then we could hijack that pile of crap the DJ's playing. . . ."

"I like the way you think. I wonder if the limo driver would mind a side trip. . . ."

Logan and Gabe ended up in a mock argument over the best CDs to retrieve—the top five were obvious, but from there down the list was a little more subjective—both of them having a better time than they'd had all evening.

It was funny, but as they joked around, Gabe had a sense that they were the *only* ones having a good time. Everyone in the room seemed to be frowning about something. And over in the corner by the stale cookies, it looked like a girl was crying. Wasn't that Evie Hess? And another girl, Ursula Tatum, also had red eyes and smeared mascara. Maybe the music and the punch weren't the only things about this prom that sucked. Clara and Bryan looked happy, but aside from those two, Gabe and Logan—both recently humiliated and rejected—seemed to be enjoying themselves more than everyone else.

Less perceptive than Gabe, Logan didn't register the negative atmosphere until Libby and Dylan started arguing; abruptly, Libby stalked off the dance floor. That caught his attention at once.

Logan shifted his weight, his eyes glued to Libby's departing figure. "Hey, Gabe, do you mind if I ditch you?"

"Not at all. Go for it."

Logan nearly sprinted after her.

Gabe wasn't sure what to do with himself now. Should he find Celeste and ask whether she minded if he bailed? He wasn't entirely comfortable with the idea of prying her loose from someone else in order to ask, though.

He decided to get another bottle of water and find the quietest corner possible to wait for the evening to drag to an end.

And then, as he went searching for that quiet corner,

Gabe felt the strange pull again, stronger than he'd ever felt it in his life; it was like someone was drowning in black waters and screaming to him for help. He glanced around frantically, wondering where the urgent call was coming from. He couldn't understand the vital, jagged edge of this distress. It was like nothing he'd ever felt before.

For just a moment, his eyes locked on one girl—on her back, as she was walking away from him. The girl's hair was black and glossy, with a mirrorlike sheen. She wore a spectacular floor-length dress the color of flames. As Gabe watched, her earrings flashed once, like little red sparklers.

Gabe began walking after her in an almost unconscious movement, drawn by the wrenching need that surrounded her. She turned slightly, and he got a glimpse of an unfamiliar pale, aquiline profile—full ivory lips and black slanting brows—before she ducked through the ladies' room door.

Gabe was breathing hard with the effort of not following the girl into no-man's-land. He could feel her need sucking at him like quicksand. He leaned against the wall across from the bathroom, folded his arms tight across his chest, and tried to talk himself out of waiting for the girl. This lunatic instinct he had was way off base. Wasn't Celeste proof of that? It was all just imagination.

Maybe he should leave now.

But Gabe couldn't force his feet to move one step away.

Though the girl barely reached five foot three inches in her stiletto heels, something about her figure—whip-slender and rod-straight as a fencing foil—made her appear tall.

She was a walking contradiction in more ways than height—both dark and light with her inky hair and chalky skin, both delicate and hard with her tiny, sharp features, and both inviting and repellent with the mesmerizing undulations of her body under the hostile expression on her face.

Only one thing about her was not ambiguous—her dress was, without question, a work of art: Bright red tongues of leather flame bared her pale shoulders and licked down her willowy curves until they kissed the floor. As she crossed the dance floor, female eyes followed the pathway of the dress with envy and male eyes followed it with lust.

There was another phenomenon that followed her; as the girl in the fiery dress passed through the dancers, little gasps of horror and pain and embarrassment rippled out from around her in strange eddies that could only be coincidence. A high heel cracked, twisting the ankle inside it. A satin dress split along a seam from thigh to waist. A contact lens popped out and was lost on the dirty floor. A vital bra strap snapped in two. A wallet slipped from a pocket. An unexpected cramp announced an early period. A borrowed necklace scattered in a shower of pearls to the floor.

And on and on—little disasters spinning small circles of misery.

The pale dark girl smiled to herself as if she could somehow sense that misery in the air and enjoy it—taste it, perhaps, considering the way she licked her lips in appreciation.

And then she frowned, furrowing her brow in fierce concentration. The one boy who was watching her face saw a strange red glitter near her earlobes, like shooting red sparks. Everyone else turned just then to stare at Brody Farrow, who clutched his arm and shouted in pain; the slight movement of the slow dancing had dislocated his shoulder.

The girl in the red dress smirked.

With her heels ringing sharply against the tile floor, she strode down the hall to the ladies' room. Faint moans of pain and chagrin trailed after her.

A crowd of girls hovered in front of the wall-length mirrors inside the bathroom. They only had a moment to gape at the stunning dress, to notice how the slight girl inside it shivered briefly in the stuffy, too-warm room, before the chaos distracted them. It started with

Emma Roland stabbing herself in the eye with a mascara
wand. She flailed in dismay, striking the full glass of
punch in Bethany Crandall's hand, which then drenched
Bethany and stained three other dresses in the most
inconvenient places. The atmosphere in the restroom
was suddenly hotter than the temperature as one girl—
sporting a hideous green smear across her chest—
accused Bethany of throwing the punch on her
purposely.

The pale dark girl only smiled slightly at the brewing
fight, and then strode to the farthest stall in the long
room and locked the door behind her.

She did not make use of the privacy the way one
might expect. Instead—showing no fear of the less-
than-sterile environment—the girl leaned her forehead
against the metal wall and squeezed her eyes shut. Her
hands, balled into sharp little fists, also rested against the
metal as if for support.

If any of the girls in the ladies' room had been paying attention, they might have wondered what was causing the red glow that shone dully through the crack
between the door and the wall. But no one was paying
attention.

The girl in the red dress clenched her teeth tightly
together. From between them, a hot spurt of bright
flame shot out and singed black patterns into the thin
layer of tan paint on the metal wall. She started to pant,

struggling with an invisible weight, and the fire burned hotter, thick fingers of red crackling against the cold metal. The fire reached up to her hair, but did not scorch the smooth, inky locks. Traces of smoke began to seep from her nose and ears.

A shower of sparks popped from her ears as she whispered one word through her teeth.

"*Melissa.*"

Back out on the crowded dance floor, Melissa Harris looked up, distracted. Had someone just called her name? There didn't seem to be anyone close enough to be responsible for the low sound. Just her imagination, then. Melissa looked back at her date and tried to concentrate on what he was saying.

Melissa wondered why she had agreed to go to the prom with Cooper Silverdale. He wasn't her type. A small boy, consumed with his own importance, with too much to prove. He'd been oddly hyper all night, bragging about his family and his possessions nonstop, and Melissa was tired of it.

Another faint whisper caught Melissa's attention, and she turned.

There, too far across the crowd to be the source behind the sound, Tyson Bell was staring straight at Melissa over the head of the girl he danced with. Melissa looked down at once, shuddering, trying not to care who he was with, forcing herself not to look.

She moved closer to Cooper. Boring and shallow, maybe, but better than Tyson. Anyone was better than Tyson.

Really? Is Cooper really the better option? The questions popped into Melissa's thoughts as if they came from someone else entirely. Involuntarily, she glanced up into Tyson's heavily lashed dark eyes. He was still staring.

Of course Cooper was better than Tyson, no matter how beautiful Tyson was. That beauty was just part of the trap.

Cooper babbled on, stumbling over his words as he tried to capture Melissa's interest.

You're out of Cooper's league, the thought whispered. Melissa shook her head, embarrassed for thinking that way. It was vain. Cooper was just as good as she was, as good as any other boy.

Not as good as Tyson. Remember how it was . . .

Melissa tried to keep the images out of her mind: Tyson's warm eyes, full of longing . . . his hands, rough and soft against her skin . . . his rich voice that made even the most common words sound like poetry . . . the way just the lightest pressure of his lips against her fingers could send her pulse sprinting in her veins . . .

Her heart thumped, aching.

Deliberately, Melissa dredged up a new memory to

combat the rebel images. Tyson's iron fist smashing into the side of her face without warning—the black spots blossoming in front of her eyes—her hands bracing against the floor—vomit choking in her throat—raw pain shaking her whole body—

He was sorry. So sorry. He promised. Never again. Unwanted, the image of Tyson's coffee eyes swimming with tears clouded her vision.

Reflexively, Melissa's eyes sought Tyson. He was still staring. His forehead creased, his eyebrows pulled together, grief-stricken . . .

Melissa shuddered again.

"Are you cold? Do you want my—?" Cooper half-shrugged out of his tuxedo jacket and then stopped himself, his face flushing. "You can't be cold. It's so hot in here," he said lamely as he withdrew the offer, buttoning the jacket back into place.

"I'm fine," Melissa assured him. She forced herself to look only at his sallow, boyish face.

"This place kinda sucks," Cooper said, and Melissa nodded, happy to agree with him. "We could go to my father's country club. There's an incredible restaurant, if you're in the mood for dessert. We won't have to wait for a table. As soon as I mention my name . . ."

Melissa's attention wandered again.

Why am I here with this little snob? asked the thought that was so strangely unfamiliar in her head, though it came in her own voice. *He's a weakling. So what if he couldn't hurt a kitten? Isn't there more to love than safety? I don't feel the same need in my stomach when I look at Cooper—when I look at anyone besides Tyson. . . . I can't lie to myself. I still want him. So much. Isn't that love, that wanting?*

Melissa wished she hadn't drunk so much of that vile, burning punch. It was impossible to think clearly.

She watched as Tyson left his partner stranded and crossed the floor until he stood right in front of her—the perfect broad-shouldered football hero cliché. It was as if Cooper didn't exist there between them.

"Melissa?" he asked in his melting voice, sorrow twisting his features. "Melissa, *please*?" He held his hand out toward her, ignoring Cooper's wordless spluttering.

Yes yes yes yes yes chanted in her head.

A thousand memories of desire rocked through her. Her clouded mind buckled.

Hesitantly, Melissa nodded.

Tyson smiled in relief, in joy, and pulled her around Cooper and into his arms.

It was just so easy to go with him. Melissa's blood ran through her veins like fire.

"*Yes!*" the pale dark girl hissed, hidden in her stall, and a forked tongue of flame lit her face with red. The fire popped loud enough that someone might have noticed if the bathroom hadn't still been full of shrill voices raised in irritation.

The fire receded, and the girl took a deep breath. Her eyelids fluttered for a moment, and then closed again. Her fists tightened until the pallid skin looked like it would split over the sharp ridges of her knuckles. Her slim figure began to tremble as if she were straining to lift a mountain. Tension and determination and expectation were a nearly visible aura around her.

Whatever difficult task she had set for herself now, it was clear that completing it was more precious to her than anything else.

"*Cooper,*" she hissed, and fire poured from her mouth, her nose, her ears. Flames bathed her face.

Like you're nothing at all. Like you're invisible. Like you don't exist! Cooper trembled with fury, and the words in his head fed the rage, brought it to a boil.

You could make *her see you. You could show Tyson who the real man is.*

Automatically, his hand reached toward the heavy bulge hidden beneath his jacket at the small of his back. The shock of remembering the gun cut right through the rage, and had him blinking rapidly, like he'd just woken from a dream.

A line of goose bumps flashed down his neck. What was he doing with a gun at the prom? Was he crazy?

It was such a stupid thing, but then, what else could he do when Warren Beeds had called him on his thoughtless brag? Sure, it was true that the school's security was a joke, that anyone could sneak in anything they wanted. He'd proved that, hadn't he? But was it worth it to have a gun at his back, just to show up Warren Beeds?

He could see Melissa, her head on that stupid jock's shoulder, her eyes closed. Had she forgotten Cooper completely?

Fury bubbled again; his hand twitched toward his back.

Cooper shook his head more vigorously this time. Insanity. That wasn't why he'd brought the gun. . . . It was just a joke, a prank.

But look at Tyson. Look at that superior, smug smile on his face! Who does he think he is? His father is no more than a glorified gardener! He's not afraid I'll do something about the fact that he stole my date. He doesn't even remember that I brought her. He wouldn't be afraid of me if he did. And Melissa doesn't remember I exist.

Cooper gritted his teeth, hotly resentful again. He imagined the superior look on Tyson's face vanishing, turning to horror and fear as he stared down a gun barrel.

Cold fear snapped Cooper back to reality.

Punch. More punch, that's what I need. It's cheap, gross

stuff, but at least it's strong. A few more cups of punch, and I'll know what to do.

Taking a deep breath to steady himself, Cooper hurried to the refreshment table.

The dark girl in the bathroom scowled and shook her head with annoyance. She took two deep breaths and then whispered calming words to herself in a throaty purr.

"There's plenty of time. A little more alcohol clouding his mind, taking his will . . . patience. There's plenty still to attend to, so many other details . . ." She gritted her teeth and her eyelids fluttered again, for a longer moment this time.

"First Matt and Louisa, then Bryan and Clara," she told herself, as if she were working her way down a to-do list. "Ugh, and then that interfering Gabe! Why isn't *he* miserable yet?" She took another steadying breath. "It's time my little helper got back to work."

She pressed her fists to her temples and closed her eyes.

"*Celeste,*" she snapped.

The voice in Celeste's head was familiar, even welcome. All of her best ideas came like this lately.

Don't Matt and Louisa look cozy?

Celeste grinned toward the couple in question.

Someone having a good time? Now is that really acceptable?

"I've got to go . . ."—Celeste looked into her partner's face, searching for his name—"Derek."

The boy's fingers, creeping up her ribs, froze in shock.

"It's been fun," Celeste assured him, rubbing the back of her hand across her open mouth as if to wipe away any trace of him. She pulled herself free.

"But, Celeste . . . I thought . . ."

"Bye, now."

Celeste's smile was sharp as a razor's edge as she strutted toward Matt Franklin and his date, mousy little what's-her-name. For a brief second, she remembered her official date—squeaky-clean Gabe Christensen— and she wanted to laugh. What a nice time he must be having tonight! The humiliation she was putting him through almost made it worth coming with him, though she couldn't imagine what she'd been thinking, saying yes. Celeste shook her head at the irritating memory. Gabe had turned those innocent blue eyes on her, and— for half a minute—she'd *wanted* to say yes. She'd wanted to move closer to him. In that brief moment, she'd thought about giving up her delicious scheme and just having a nice time at the prom with a nice guy.

Wow, she was glad that goody-goody notion had faded. Celeste had never had more fun in her life than she was having now. She'd ruined prom for half the girls in the room, and had half the boys fighting over her. Boys were all the same, and they were all hers for the taking. It was time the rest of the girls saw that. What a fabulous bit of inspiration this plot for total prom domination had been!

"Hey, Matt," Celeste cooed, tapping him on the shoulder.

"Oh, hey," Matt responded, looking up from his date with a confused expression.

"Can I borrow you for a moment?" Celeste asked, batting her lashes and throwing her shoulders back to place her cleavage in the spotlight. "There's something I want to, er, *show* you." Celeste ran her tongue over her lips.

"Um." Matt swallowed loudly.

Celeste felt her last partner's eyes boring a hole in her back, and she remembered that Matt was his best friend. She stifled a laugh. How perfect.

"Matt?" his date asked in injured tones as his hands dropped from her waist.

"I'll be just a sec . . . Louisa."

Ha! He could barely remember her name himself! Celeste flashed him a dazzling smile.

"Matt?" Louisa called again, shocked and hurt, as Matt took Celeste's hand and followed her toward the center of the dance floor.

The furthest stall in the bathroom was dark now. The girl inside it slumped against the wall, waiting as her breathing slowed. Despite the fact that the air in the room was uncomfortably warm, the girl was shivering.

The quarrel in the bathroom had resolved, and a new bevy of girls crowded in front of the mirror to check their makeup.

The fire-breather composed herself, and then there was another sparkle of red at her ears; everyone at the mirror turned to look expectantly at the ladies' room door while the girl in the red dress ducked out of her stall and opened the low window. No one noticed her slip out the unorthodox exit. They continued to stare at the door, looking for the sound that had made them turn.

The sticky, humid Miami night was as uncomfortable as if it were trying to rival hell. In her thick leather dress, the girl smiled a relieved smile and rubbed her hands against her bare arms.

She let her body relax against the side of a nearby grimy Dumpster, and leaned toward the open top where the stench of rotting food hung in a heavy cloud. Her eyes slipped closed, then she inhaled deeply and smiled again.

Another, even more vile smell—something like rancid, burning flesh, but worse—wafted through the sultry air. The girl's smile widened as she sucked in this painful new odor like it was the rarest perfume.

And then her eyes snapped open and her body wrenched straight and stiff.

A low chuckle rolled out of the velvet darkness.

"Feeling homesick, Sheeb?" a woman's voice purred.

The girl's lips curled into a snarl as the body that belonged with the voice coalesced into view.

The stunning black-haired woman seemed to be clothed in nothing but a lazily swirling black mist. Her legs and feet were invisible—perhaps not even there. High on her forehead were two small, polished onyx horns.

"Chex Jezebel aut Baal-Malphus," the girl in the red dress growled. "What are you doing here?"

"So formal, little sister?"

"What do I care for sisters?"

"True. And our exact parentage *is* shared by thousands . . . But that's such an unwieldy mouthful. Why don't you just call me Jez, and I'll skip over the Chex Sheba aut Baal-Malphus and call you Sheeb."

Sheba snorted derisively. "I thought you were assigned to New York."

"Just taking a break—like you are, apparently." Jezebel looked pointedly at Sheba's resting spot. "New York is fabulous—almost as evil as hell, thanks for asking—but even the killers sleep now and then. I got bored, so I came down to see if you were having fun at the *purrrrrrrrr*-rom." Jezebel laughed. The dark mist around her danced.

Sheba scowled but did not answer.

Her mind was on alert as she focused back on the unsuspecting teenagers inside the hotel ballroom, looking for interference. Was Jezebel here to mess with Sheba's plans? What else? Most middle demons would go miles out of their way to screw over a little leaguer—to the point of doing a good deed, even. Balan Lilith Hadad aut Hamon had once disguised herself as a human at one of Sheba's assigned high schools, about a decade back. Sheba hadn't understood why all her miserable plots kept turning into happy endings. Then, when she'd figured it out, she still could hardly believe Lilith's gall—the vicious demoness had actually orchestrated three separate instances of true love, just to get Sheba demoted! Lucky for Sheba, she'd pulled off a good betrayal at the last minute that took out two of the romances. Sheba sucked in a deep breath. That had been a close one. She could have been bounced back to middle school!

Sheba grimaced at the succulent demoness floating before her now. If Sheba had a dream job like Jezebel's—

a homicide demon! It didn't get much better than that—Sheba would stick to the mayhem and forget the petty tricks.

Sheba's thoughts twisted like invisible smoke through the dancers in the building behind her, looking for any signs of treachery. But everything continued as it should. The misery in the room was reaching new heights. The flavor of human unhappiness filled her mind. Delicious.

Jezebel chuckled, understanding exactly what Sheba was doing.

"Relax," Jezebel said. "I'm not here to cause you any trouble."

Sheba snorted. Of course Jezebel was there to cause trouble. That's what demons did.

"Great dress," Jezebel noted. "Hell hound skin. Terrific for inciting lust and envy."

"I know how to do my job."

Jezebel laughed again, and Sheba leaned in instinctively to catch the brimstone flavor of her breath.

"Poor Sheeb, still locked in half-human form," Jezebel teased. "I remember how *good* everything smells all the time. Ugh. And the temperature! Do the humans have to freeze everything with their wretched air-conditioning?"

Sheba's face was smooth now, controlled. "I get by. There's plenty of misery to go around."

"That's the spirit! Just another few centuries, and

you'll be in the big-time with me."

Sheba allowed a smirk to curl her lips. "Or maybe not quite so long."

One black eyebrow arched high against Jezebel's white forehead, raising almost to an ebony horn.

"Is that so? Got something particularly evil up your sleeve, little sister?"

Sheba didn't answer, tensing again as Jezebel sent her own thoughts snaking invisibly through the crowd inside the ballroom. Sheba locked her jaw, ready to strike back if Jezebel tried to undo any of her schemes. But Jezebel just looked, touching nothing.

"Hmm," Jezebel hummed to herself. "Hmm."

Sheba's fists clenched hard as Jezebel's search touched Cooper Silverdale, but again, Jezebel merely observed.

"Well, well," the horned demoness murmured. "Wow. Sheeb, I've got to say it, I'm impressed. You got a *gun* in. And a motivated hand—full of alcohol to weaken his free will!" The older demoness smiled with something that looked strangely like sincerity. "This is really evil. I mean, sure, a middle demon working homicide or mayhem or maybe riots could set something like this up at a prom, but a human-form child on misery detail? What are you, two, three hundred?"

"Just one-eighty-six at my last spawn day," Sheba answered brusquely, still wary.

Jezebel whistled a tongue of flame through her lips. "Very impressed. And I can see that you aren't neglecting your assignment, either. That's one miserable crowd in there." Jezebel laughed. "You've ended nearly every promising relationship, broken a few dozen lifelong friendships, made new enemies . . . three, four, *five* fights brewing," Jezebel counted, her mind with the humans. "You've even got the DJ listening to you! Such attention to detail. Ha-ha! I can count on one hand the humans who aren't completely wretched."

Sheba smiled grimly. "I'll get to them."

"Ghastly, Sheeb. Seriously nasty. You do our name proud. If every prom had a demoness like you involved, we'd own this world."

"Aw, Jez, you're making me blush," Sheba said with heavy sarcasm.

Jezebel laughed. "Of course, you've got a little help."

Jezebel's thoughts twisted in a circle around Celeste, who had just twisted herself around a new boy. Jilted girls cried, while the boys Celeste carelessly tossed aside flexed their fists and glowered wrathfully at their competition; burning with lust, each was determined that Celeste was finishing the night with him.

Celeste was doing half the work tonight.

"I use the tools available to me," Sheba said.

"What an ironic name! What an evil mind! Is she fully human?"

"I passed her in the hall, just to check," Sheba admitted. "Pure, clean human scent. Revolting."

"Huh. I would have sworn she had some demon in her ancestry. Good find. But, Sheba, asking a date? Pretty amateur, involving yourself physically that way."

Sheba's chin jabbed upward defensively, but she did not answer. Jezebel was right; it was crude and time-consuming to use one's human form rather than one's demon mind. However, it was the results that counted. Sheba's timely interference had kept Logan from discovering his true love.

"Well, it in no way diminishes your accomplishments here tonight." Jezebel's tone was conciliatory. "You pull this one off, and they'll put you in the baby demons' textbooks."

"Thanks," Sheba snapped. Did Jezebel really think she could flatter Sheba into letting her guard down?

Jezebel smiled, and her mists curled up on the edges, mirroring the expression.

"A tip, Sheba. Keep them confused in there. If you can get Cooper to pull the trigger, then you might make some of these wannabe gangsters think they're under fire." Jezebel shook her head in wonder. "You've got so much potential mayhem here. Of course, they'll bring in a riot demon if it really gets hot . . . but you'd still get some of the credit for stirring it up."

Sheba grimaced, and glimmers of red flashed at her

ears. What was Jezebel doing? Where was the trick? Her mind ran over and over the humans she was assigned to torment, but she could find no trace of Jezebel's distinct brimstone flavor in the ballroom. There was nothing but the misery Sheba had caused herself, and the few little pockets of repellent happiness that Sheba would attend to shortly.

"You're certainly *helpful* tonight," Sheba said, being deliberately insulting.

Jezebel sighed, and there was something about the way her mists rolled back in on themselves that made her look . . . embarrassed. For the first time, Sheba felt a hint of doubt about her assumptions. But Jezebel's motives *had* to be malicious. That's the only kind of motives demons had.

With a rueful expression on her face, Jezebel asked quietly, "Is it so impossible to believe that I might want you to get promoted?"

"*Yes.*"

Jezebel sighed again. And again, the way her mists writhed in chagrin made Sheba uncertain.

"Why?" Sheba demanded. "What do you get out of this?"

"I know it's all wrong—or rather right—for me to be giving you advice you can work with. Not very evil of me."

Sheba nodded cautiously.

"It's in our nature to trip up everyone, demons, humans—even angels if we get the chance. We're evil. Naturally we're going to backstab, whether it hurts our side or not. We wouldn't be demons if we didn't let envy, greed, lust, and wrath rule us." Jezebel chuckled. "I remember—how many years ago was it?—Lilith almost got you booted back a few grades, didn't she?"

Red fire smoldered in Sheba's eyes at the memory. "Almost."

"You handled it better than most. You're one of the very worst working misery right now, you know."

Flattery again? Sheba stiffened.

Jezebel twisted her mists up with a finger, and then circled that finger so that the mists drew a smoky orb against the night sky.

"There's a bigger picture, though, Sheba. Demons like Lilith can't see past the evil at hand. But there's a whole world out there, full of humans making millions of decisions every minute of the day and night. We can only be there to sway a fraction of those decisions. And sometimes, well, from where I'm standing, it feels like the angels are getting ahead. . . ."

"But, Jezebel!" Sheba gasped, shock breaking through her suspicion. "We're winning. Just watch the news—it's *obvious* we're winning."

"I know, I know. But even with all the wars and destruction . . . it's odd, Sheba. There's still an awful lot of happiness out there. For every mugging I turn into a homicide, across town some angel has a bystander jumping another mugger to save the day. Or convincing the mugger to give up his wicked ways! Ugh. We're losing ground."

"But the angels are weak, Jezebel. Everyone knows that. They're so full of love that they can't concentrate. Half the time the stupid birdbrains fall in love with a human and trade their wings for a human body. Though why even an idiot angel would want this!" Sheba scowled down the length of her human form. So limiting. "I've never really understood the point of having to wear these around for half a millennium. I guess it's probably just to torture us, isn't it? The dark lords must enjoy watching us squirm."

"It's more than that. It's to make you really *hate* them. The humans, I mean."

Sheba stared at her. "Why would I need a reason? Hate is what I *do*."

"It happens, you know," Jezebel said slowly. "The angels aren't the only ones to give it all up. There are demons who've traded their horns for a human."

"No!" Sheba's eyes widened, then narrowed in disbelief. "You're exaggerating. Now and then a demon shacks up with a human, but it's just to torment them. Just a bit of malicious fun."

Jezebel winced, swishing her mists into figure eights,

but she didn't argue back. That's what made Sheba realize she was serious.

Sheba swallowed hard. "Wow."

She couldn't imagine that. Taking all this delicious evil and throwing it away. Giving up a hard-earned pair of horns—horns that Sheba would destroy anything to have right now—and getting stuck with a weak, fully mortal body in return.

Sheba eyed Jezebel's glistening onyx horns and frowned. "I don't understand how anyone could do that."

"Remember what you said about the angels? Getting distracted by love?" Jezebel asked. "Well, hate can be a distraction, too. Look at Lilith and her spiteful good deeds. Maybe it starts out with sticking it to the lesser demons, but who knows where it will lead? Virtue corrupts."

"I can't believe a few tricks against another demon could make you as stupid as a *birdbrain*," Sheba mumbled under her breath.

"Sheba, don't underestimate the angels," Jezebel chastised. "You don't mess with them—you hear? Even a strong middle demon like me knows better than to lock horns with the feather-backs. They steer clear of us, and we steer clear of them. Let the Demon Lords deal with the angels."

"I know that, Jezebel. I wasn't spawned this decade."

"Sorry. I'm being helpful again." She shuddered. "I just get so frustrated sometimes! Goodness and light on every side!"

Sheba shook her head. "I don't see that. Misery is everywhere."

"Happiness is, too, sis. It's all over the place," Jezebel said sadly.

It was silent for a long moment as Jezebel's words lingered in the air. The sticky breeze washed across Sheba's skin. Miami was no hell, but it was comfortable at least.

"Not at my prom!" Sheba retorted with sudden fierceness.

Jezebel smiled widely—her teeth were black as the night sky. "That's just it—that's why I'm being so undamnedly helpful. Because we need demonesses like you out there. We need the worst we can get on the front lines. Let the Liliths of the underworld mess around with petty tricks. Get me the Shebas on my side. Get me a thousand Shebas. We'll win this fight once and for all."

Sheba considered that for a moment, weighing the fierce purpose in Jezebel's voice. "That's evil in such a strange way. It almost sounds like good."

"Twisted, I know."

They laughed together for the first time.

"Well, get back in there and destroy that prom."

"I'm on it. Go to hell, Jezebel."

"Thanks, Sheeb. Back at you."

Jezebel winked once, and then smiled wider until the black of her teeth seemed to envelop her entire face. She evaporated into the night.

Sheba lingered in the dirty alley until the alluring scent of brimstone had faded away entirely, and then break time was over. Invigorated by the idea of joining the front lines, Sheba hurried back to her misery.

The prom was in full swing, and everything was falling into place.

Celeste was scoring high in her malicious game; she awarded herself a point for every girl who cried in a dark corner of the ballroom. Two points for every boy who threw a punch at a rival.

All over the room, the seeds Sheba had planted were flowering. Hate was blooming alongside lust and rage and despair. A garden straight from hell.

Sheba enjoyed it all from behind a potted palm.

No, she couldn't *force* the humans to do anything. They had their innate free will, and so she could only tempt, could only suggest. Little things—high heels and seams and minor muscle groups—she could manipulate physically, but she could never force their minds. They had to choose to listen. And tonight, they were listening.

Sheba was on a roll, and she didn't want any loose ends, so before she turned back to her most ambitious scheme—Cooper was pliant with intoxication now, ready for her direction—she sent her thoughts searching through the crowd for those small, annoying bubbles of happiness.

No one was walking away from this prom unscathed. Not while Sheba had a spark in her body.

Over there—what was this? Bryan Walker and Clara Hurst were staring dreamily into each other's eyes, totally oblivious to the wrath and despair and bad music surrounding them, just enjoying each other's company.

Sheba considered her options and decided to have Celeste interfere. Celeste should enjoy that—nothing was more evilly fun than flaunting your power right in the face of a pure romance. Besides, Celeste listened to every suggestion Sheba fed her, entirely agreeable to any demonic scheme.

Sheba continued with her evaluation before acting.

Not too far away, Sheba found that she'd dropped the ball in an inexcusable fashion. Was that her own date, Logan, actually *enjoying* himself? Impossible. So, he'd found his Libby after all and they were both unacceptably happy. Well, that would be easy enough to rectify. She'd go reclaim her partner and send Libby running away in tears. Amateur and crude to intervene bodily . . . Still, better that than let happiness win even one small battle.

Sheba's assessment was almost done. There was just one more tiny pocket of peace—not a couple this time;

it was a lone boy wandering into the far end of the room from the hall. That annoying Gabe Christensen.

Sheba scowled in his direction. What did *he* have to be happy about? He was rejected and alone. His date was the scourge of the prom. A normal boy would be full of rage or pain right now. But he insisted on making more work for her!

Sheba inspected Gabe's mind more closely. Hmm. Gabe wasn't really *happy*. In fact, he was worrying intensely at the moment, searching for someone. Celeste was quite clearly in his view, writhing to a slow song with Rob Carlton (Pamela Green watched the display with shocked eyes, despair leaking deliciously into the air around her), but she wasn't the source of Gabe's worry. There was someone else he wanted to find.

So he wasn't happy—that wasn't the sensation that had trespassed on Sheba's atmosphere of misery. It was *goodness* itself that was exuding from this boy. Even worse.

Sheba ducked behind the palm and pushed out with her thoughts. Smoke oozed from her nose. "*Gabe.*"

Gabe shook his head absently and continued with his search.

He'd waited half an hour as throngs of girls left the bathroom, drove after drove. Here and there Gabe had felt a weak pull, but nothing at all like that one girl's raging, suffocating need.

When three separate groups had all come and gone, Gabe had stopped Jill Stein to ask after the girl.

"Black hair and a red dress? No, I didn't see anyone like that in there. I think the bathroom is empty."

The girl must have slipped past him somehow.

Gabe had just returned to the dance floor, brooding over the mystery girl. At least Bryan and Clara and Logan and Libby were having fun. That was good. The rest of the class seemed to be having an exceptionally nasty evening.

And then, there it was again. Gabe's head jerked up, feeling the desperation he'd been searching for. Where *was* she?

Sheba hissed in frustration. The boy's mind was entirely sober and singularly closed to her insidious voice. Well, that wasn't going to stop her. She had other tools.

"Celeste."

It was time the evil girl tormented her own date.

Sheba leaned lightly on Celeste, suggesting that avenue. After all, Gabe was attractive by human standards. Certainly good enough for Celeste, whose standards were hardly rigorous. Gabe was tall and subtly muscular, with dark hair and symmetrical features. He had pale blue eyes that Sheba personally found a bit repulsive—they were so decidedly un-damned, almost *heavenly*, ugh!—but that appealed to mortal girls. It was looking into those clear eyes that had made Celeste say yes to this squeaky clean do-gooder's invitation.

Do-gooder, indeed. Sheba's eyes narrowed. Gabe had already been on her list before he insisted on disregarding her here at the prom. This was the very boy who had ruined her plans for the lecherous math teacher—just a little bit of pre-prom fun Sheba had arranged in between making sure that everyone asked exactly the wrong person to the big dance. If Gabe hadn't confronted Mr. Reese at a critical moment of temptation . . . Sheba gritted her teeth and sparks flickered out of her ears. She would have ruined the man and the impossibly innocent girl, too. Not that Mr. Reese had had far to fall, but it would have been a fantastic scandal. And now the math teacher was being especially careful, made wary by those same sky-blue eyes. Feeling *guilty*, even. Considering counseling for his problem. Ugh!

Gabe Christensen owed Sheba some misery. She would get her due.

Sheba glared at Celeste, wondering why the girl had made no move toward her date. Celeste was still wrapped around Rob, enjoying Pamela's pain. Enough fun! There was havoc to be wreaked. Sheba whispered suggestions in Celeste's mind, nudging her in Gabe's direction.

Celeste shrugged away from Rob and glanced toward

Gabe, who was still combing through the crowd with his gaze. Her brown eyes settled on his blue for just a second, and then she moved, *cringed* actually, back into Rob's arms.

Odd. Gabe's light eyes seemed to be almost as repellent to the vicious blonde as they were to Sheba.

Sheba leaned again, but Celeste—for once—shook her off, trying to distract herself from thoughts of Gabe with Rob's eager lips.

Baffled, Sheba cast around for another avenue to destroy the irritating boy, but she was interrupted by something much more important than one good human.

Cooper Silverdale was simply quivering with rage on one side of the dance floor, glowering at Melissa and Tyson. Melissa had her head on Tyson's shoulder and was oblivious to the smug grin Tyson aimed in Cooper's direction.

It was time to act. Cooper was considering another glass of punch to drown his pain, and he was much too close to passing out for Sheba to allow that. She focused on him, smoke at her ears, and Cooper realized dully that the green punch was revolting. He couldn't stand any more. He threw his half-empty cup to the floor and turned back to glare at Tyson.

She thinks I'm pathetic, said the voice in Cooper's head. *No, she doesn't even think of me at all. But I can make it so she'll never be able to forget me. . . .*

His head thick with alcohol, Cooper reached back and stroked his hand along the barrel of the gun under his jacket.

Sheba held her breath. Sparks flew from her ears.

And then, in that vital second, Sheba was distracted by the knowledge that someone was staring intensely at her own face.

Here, in the ballroom, that same sucking need, pulling at him—someone drowning, shrieking for help. It had to be the same girl. Gabe had never felt anything so urgent in his life.

His eyes raked desperately over the couples on the floor, but he couldn't see her. He paced the edge of the floor, searching the faces of the people on the sidelines. She wasn't there, either.

He saw Celeste with yet another boy, but his eyes didn't pause. If Celeste didn't claim her ride home soon, there wasn't much he could do about it. Someone else needed Gabe more.

The need tugged at him again, yanked hard, and for a moment, Gabe wondered if he was going crazy. Maybe he'd only imagined the girl in the fiery dress. Maybe this sense of frenzied need was just the onset of some delusion.

At that moment, Gabe's seeking eyes found what they were searching for.

Stepping around Heath McKenzie's big sulking form, Gabe's eyes locked on a tiny, but brilliant, red flash. There she was—half-hidden behind a fake tree, her earrings glinting like sparklers again—the girl in the red dress. Her dark eyes, deep as the pool he'd imagined her drowning in, met his. The vibrant need was an aura surrounding her. He didn't have to think about moving toward her. There was probably no way he could have stopped himself if he'd wanted to.

He was sure he'd never seen this girl before tonight; she was completely unfamiliar.

Her dark, almond-shaped eyes were composed and careful, but at the same time they cried out to him. They were the focus of the need he felt. He could no more resist their plea than he could tell his heart to stop beating.

She needed him.

Sheba watched with disbelief as Gabe Christensen walked straight toward her. She saw her own face in his head and realized that the person Gabe had been looking for was . . . Sheba.

She allowed the brief distraction—knowing that Cooper was hers for the taking, that a few minutes' time wouldn't save him now—and rejoiced in the delicious irony. So Gabe wanted to be ruined by Sheba personally? Well, she would oblige him. It would make his misery even sweeter knowing that he'd chosen it himself. She straightened up in her hell-hound dress, letting it caress her figure suggestively. She knew what any human male would have to feel when he examined *this* dress.

But the exasperating boy was focused on her eyes.

It was dangerous to look straight into the eyes of a demoness. Humans who didn't look away fast enough could get trapped there. And then they were stuck, pining after the demoness forever, burning for her . . .

Biting back a smile, Sheba met his gaze, staring deep into his sky-colored eyes. Silly human.

Gabe stopped a few short feet from the girl, close enough that he wouldn't have to shout over the loud music. He knew he was staring too intently—she would think he was rude, or some kind of freak. But she stared back, just as intent, her deep eyes probing his.

He opened his mouth to introduce himself, when suddenly the girl's careful expression melted into one of shock. Shock? Or horror? Her pale lips fell apart, and he heard a little gasp escape them. Her stiff posture crumpled, and she began to collapse.

Gabe jumped toward her and caught her in his arms before she could fall.

Sheba's knees buckled when her fires went out. Her internal flame died, sucked dry, snuffed like a candle in a vacuum.

The room was not so cold anymore, and she could smell nothing more than sweat, cologne, and stale, conditioned air. She could no longer taste the delicious misery she'd created. She couldn't taste anything but her own dry mouth.

But she could feel the strong arms of Gabe Christensen holding her up.

The girl's dress was soft and warm. Maybe that was the problem, Gabe thought as he pulled her toward him. Maybe the heat of the crowded room was too much combined with her heavy dress. Anxiously, Gabe brushed the silky hair away from her face. Her forehead seemed cool enough and her soft skin wasn't clammy with sweat. All the while, her stunned eyes never wavered from his.

"Are you okay? Can you stand? I'm sorry, I don't know your name."

"I'm fine," the girl said in a low, purring voice. Despite the purr, her voice was just as stunned as her eyes. "I . . . I can stand."

She straightened up, but Gabe didn't let her go. He didn't want to. And she wasn't pulling away. Her small hands had crept up to rest on his shoulders, like they were dancing partners.

"Who *are* you?" she asked in that throaty voice.

"Gabe—Gabriel Michael Christensen," he elaborated with a grin. "And you are?"

"Sheba," she said, her dark eyes widening. "Sheba . . . Smith."

"Well, would you like to dance then, Sheba Smith? If you feel well enough."

"Yes," she breathed, half to herself. "Yes, why not?"

Her eyes never left his.

Not moving from where they were, Gabe and Sheba began swaying to the rhythm of yet another wretched song. This time, the horrid music didn't offend Gabe as much.

Gabe put it together then. New girl. Amazing dress. Sheba. This was Logan's date, the one who'd asked him to the prom and then wanted nothing more to do with him. For a half second, Gabe worried if it was wrong for him to infringe on his friend's date. But the worry passed quickly.

For one thing, Logan was happy with Libby. There was no sense in interrupting something that was clearly meant to be.

For another, Sheba and Logan were clearly *not* meant to be.

Gabe had always had a good instinct for that—for the personalities that belonged together, for compatible natures that would pull together harmoniously. He'd been the butt of many jokes about matchmaking, but he didn't mind. Gabe liked people to be happy.

And this intense girl with the deep pools in her eyes—Sheba—did not belong with Logan.

That desperate sense of need had calmed when he'd touched her. Gabe felt much better with her in his arms—holding her seemed to soothe the strange call. She was safe here, no longer drowning, no longer lost. Gabe was afraid to let her go, worried that the burning need would return.

It was an odd first for Gabe, this feeling of being in exactly the right place, of being the only one that belonged here. It wasn't that he'd never had a girlfriend before—girls liked Gabe, and he'd had many casual relationships. But they never lasted. There was always someone else they belonged with. None of them really needed Gabe, except as a friend. And they'd always stayed good friends.

It had never been like this. Was this where Gabe belonged? Shielding this slender girl, holding her safe in his arms?

It was silly to think so fatalistically. Gabe tried hard to act normal.

"You're new at Reed River, aren't you?" he asked her.

"I've only been here a few weeks," she confirmed.

"I don't think we have any classes together."

"No, I would have remembered if I'd been close to *you* before."

It was an odd way of phrasing it. She stared into his eyes, her hands clinging gently to his shoulders. Instinctively, he pulled her a little closer.

"Are you having a good time tonight?" he asked.

She sighed, a deep sigh from the center of her being. "I am now," she said, oddly rueful. "A very *good* time."

Trapped! Like an idiot, like a new-spawned whelp, a novice, a rookie!

Sheba leaned into Gabe, unable to resist. Unable to *want* to resist. She stared into his heavenly eyes and had the most ridiculous urge to sigh.

How had she not seen the signs?

The way goodness itself surrounded him like a shield. The way her suggestions bounced right off him harmlessly. The way the only ones safe from her evil tonight—those little bubbles of happiness outside of her control—were the people he'd touched and interacted with, his friends.

The eyes alone should have been warning enough!

Celeste was smarter than Sheba. At least her instincts had kept her away from this dangerous boy. Once she was free of his piercing gaze, she'd kept a safe distance between them. Why hadn't Sheba understood the reason behind this? And the reason Gabe had chosen Celeste in the first place. Of course he'd been drawn to Celeste! It all made sense now.

Sheba swayed to the beat that rumbled through the air, feeling the security of his body around her, protecting her. Tiny, unfamiliar tendrils of happiness twisted their way through her empty core.

No—not that! Not happiness!

If she was already feeling happy, then better things couldn't be too far behind. Was there no way to avoid the horrible wonder of *love*?

That wasn't very likely when you were in an angel's arms.

Not a true angel. Gabe didn't have wings, he'd never had them—he wasn't one of those sappy birdbrains who'd traded feathers and eternity for human love. But one of his parents had done just that.

Gabe was fully half-angel—though he didn't have a clue about his nature. If he'd had any idea, Sheba would have heard that in his mind and escaped this divine horror. Now it was only too obvious to Sheba—this close, she could smell the scent of asphodel clinging to his skin. And, clearly, he'd inherited his angel-parent's eyes. The heaven-blue eyes that should have been a dead giveaway, if Sheba hadn't been so wrapped up in her evil plotting.

There was a reason even experienced demons like Jezebel were wary of angels. If it was hazardous for a human to stare into a demon's eyes, it was doubly so for a demon to get locked into an angel's. If ever a demon met an angel's gaze for too long, *pfffffft!*—out went the fires of hell and the demon was trapped until the angel gave up on saving him.

Because that's what angels did. They *saved*.

Sheba was an eternal being, and she was trapped for however long Gabe decided to keep her.

A full angel would have known what Sheba was at once, and driven her out if he were strong enough, or given her a wide berth if he wasn't. But Sheba could imagine what her presence would feel like to someone with Gabe's instinct to save. Innocent of the knowledge he needed to understand, Sheba's damned state must have been like a siren's call.

She stared helplessly into Gabe's beautiful face, her body filling with happiness, and wondered how long the torture would last.

Already too long to save her perfect prom.

Without her hellfire, Sheba had no influence over the mortals here. But she was still fully aware, watching helpless and disgustingly blissful, as it all fell apart.

Cooper Silverdale gasped in horror as he looked at the gun glistening in his shaking hand. What was he *thinking*? He shoved the weapon back into its hiding place and half ran to the bathroom, where he violently vomited the punch into the sink.

Cooper's stomach problems interrupted Matt and

Derek's fistfight, which was just warming up in the men's room. The two friends squinted through their swollen eyes at each other. Why were they fighting? Over a girl that neither of them even liked? How stupid! Suddenly, they were interrupting each other in their urgent need to apologize. With smiles on split lips and arms around shoulders, they headed back to the ball-room.

David Alvarado had given up his plans to jump Heath after the dance, because Evie had forgiven him for disappearing with Celeste. Her cheek was soft and warm against his now as they swayed to the slow music, and there was no way he would hurt her by disappearing again, not for any reason.

David was not the only one who felt that way. As if the new song was magical rather than insipid, the dancers in the big ballroom each moved instinctively toward the person they should have come with in the first place, the one that would transform the night's misery into happiness.

Coach Lauder, lonely and depressed, looked up from the unappetizing cookies straight into Vice Principal Finkle's sad eyes. She looked lonely, too. The coach walked toward her, smiling hesitantly.

Shaking her head and blinking her eyes like someone trying to escape a nightmare, Melissa Harris pulled away from Tyson and ran for the exit. She would find the concierge and get a cab . . .

Like a rubber band that had been stretched too far, the atmosphere at Reed River's prom now snapped back with a vengeance. If Sheba had been herself, she would have pulled that rubber band until it exploded into pieces. But now all the misery and wrath and hate vanished. The human minds had been stuck in their grip too long. With relief, everyone at the prom relaxed into happiness, grasped at love with two hands.

Even Celeste was tired of the mayhem. She stayed in Rob's arms, shuddering slightly at the memory of those perfect blue eyes, as one slow song melted into the next.

Neither Sheba nor Gabe even noticed the song change.

All her delicious pain and misery destroyed! Even if she did get free, Sheba was destined for middle school now. Where was the injustice?!

And Jezebel! Had she planned this? Tried to distract Sheba from the fact that a dangerous half-angel was here tonight? Or would she be disappointed? Was she really there in encouragement? Sheba had no way to find out. She wouldn't even be able to see Jezebel now—whether the horned demoness was laughing or chagrined—with her fires extinguished.

Disgusted with herself, Sheba sighed in happiness.

Gabe was just so *good*. And, in his arms, she felt good, too. She felt wonderful.

Sheba simply had to get free before happiness and love ruined her! Would she be trapped with some feather-back's heavenly offspring forever?

Gabe smiled at her, and she sighed again.

Sheba knew what Gabe would be feeling now. Angels were never happier than when they were making someone else happy, and the bigger the lift in that other person's spirit, the more ecstatic the angel. As perfectly miserable and damned as Sheba had been, Gabe must be flying now—it would be almost as good as having wings. He would never want to let her go.

There was just one chance left for Sheba, just one way back to her wretched, miserable, burning, stinking home.

Gabe had to order her there.

Thinking of this chance, Sheba felt much worse, felt a welcome wave of her former misery. Gabe tightened his hold on her as he sensed her slipping down, and the misery was drowned in contentment, but Sheba remained hopeful.

She stared up into his love-filled angel-eyes and smiled dreamily.

You're evil incarnate, Sheba told herself. *You have a true talent for misery. You know suffering inside and out.*

You can get yourself out of this trap and everything will be like it used to be.

After all, with as much pain and havoc as Sheba was capable of causing, how hard could it possibly be to get this angelic boy to tell her to go to hell?

A hilarious new novel about getting in trouble, getting caught, and getting the guy, from #1 nationally bestselling author Meg Cabot

#1 NATIONAL BESTSELLING AUTHOR

MEG CABOT

Pants on Fire

Katie Ellison has everything going for her senior year—a great job, two boyfriends, and a good shot at being crowned Quahog Princess of her small coastal town in Connecticut. So why does Tommy Sullivan have to come back into her life? Sure, they used to be friends, but that was before the huge screwup that turned their whole town against him. Now he's back, and making Katie's perfect life a total disaster. Can the Quahog Princess and the *freak* have anything in common? Could they even be falling for each other?

HARPER TEEN
An Imprint of HarperCollins Publishers

www.harperteen.com

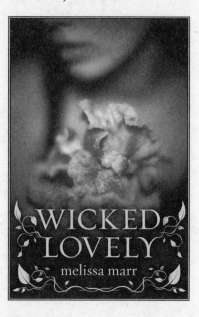

36%
Las Vegas mystery

49%
unstoppable crush

15%
fashion emergency

100%
THE CAT'S FAULT

Jasmine Callihan is just minding her own business at the hotel pool when she is tangled in a badly misbehaving pet cat's leash and tossed headlong into mystery, intrigue, and romance. With all the glitz of Las Vegas and a ridiculously entertaining cast of characters, Michele Jaffe's *Bad Kitty* is the story of seventeen-year-old Jasmine's mostly well-dressed, sometimes thrilling, but always entertaining vacation in Sin City.